BREAKING THE GREEK'S RULES

BY

ANNE McALLISTER

MILLS BOON

First published in Great Britain 2012
by Mills & Boon, an imprint of Harlequin (UK) Limited.
Large Print edition 2013
Harlequin (UK) Limited, Eton House,
18-24 Paradise Road, Richmond, Surrey TW9 1SR

© Barbara Schenck 2012

ISBN: 978 0 263 23670 5

Harlequin (UK) policy is to use papers that are natural,
renewable and recyclable products and made from
wood grown in sustainable forests. The logging and
manufacturing process conform to the legal environmental
regulations of the country of origin.

Printed and bound in Great Britain
by CPI Antony Rowe, Chippenham, Wiltshire

BREAKING THE GREEK'S RULES

For Nancy

CHAPTER ONE

ALEXANDROS Antonides studied the crumpled receipt, the one with the hastily scrawled name, address and phone number on the back, and was tempted to stuff it right back in his pocket.

Or better yet, throw it out.

He didn't need a matchmaker, for God's sake!

His fingers crushed the already frequently crumpled piece of paper and he stared out the window of the taxi as it headed north on Eighth Avenue. They weren't out of midtown Manhattan yet. It was nearly five-thirty. He should just tell the driver to forget it.

But he didn't. Instead he made himself lean back against the seat and, just as he had done a dozen or more times before, he smoothed out the paper against his palm.

Daisy Connolly. His cousin Lukas had scribbled down her name and address a month ago when he and Lukas had met up at the family reunion out at Lukas's parents' place in the Hamptons. "She'll find you the perfect wife."

"How do you know?" he'd asked Lukas, letting his voice carry his obvious doubt. He'd looked around pointedly, noting Lukas's complete lack of not only a wife, but even a date for their family reunion.

"Seen her do it," Lukas said frankly. "I went to college with her. She did it then. She does it now. She has some uncanny sense of who belongs together." He shrugged. "Who knows how she does it? Hocus-pocus? Tea leaves? Beats me. Give her a call or go see her."

Alex had grunted, not a sound meant to convey agreement.

"Unless you really don't want to get married." Lukas had cocked his head, considering Alex. Then, "Maybe he's chicken," he had said to his brothers.

One of them had made a clucking sound.

Alex had masked his irritation and rolled his eyes. "Fine," he'd said curtly. "If I get desperate enough, I'll look her up."

"I'd say you're already desperate," Lukas had said, grinning. "How many fiancées have you gone through?"

"Two," Alex said through his teeth. "But Imogene doesn't count."

Imogene had been perfect. She hadn't loved Alex any more than he'd loved her. When her long-time boyfriend had got cold feet faced with a lifetime commitment, Alex had grabbed her on the rebound. Unfortunately two days after she'd said yes to Alex, the love of her life had come to his senses and begged her to marry him.

"What can I do?" she'd wailed at Alex. "I still love him!"

The more fool she, Alex had thought. But he'd been polite and wished her good luck. He still did. If she was that besotted, she'd need it.

"I don't know," Lukas had said slowly, studying him. "Two fiancées in a little over a year…" He'd arched his brows in speculation, then looked over at his brothers. "Sounds pretty desperate to me."

His brothers, Elias and PJ, had nodded sagely.

Alex had merely snorted. He didn't want a perfect wife, anyway. He just wanted a suitable one. He was thirty-five years old. Time to get married.

Of course lots of men would disagree. But not Antonides men. Antonides men married. All of them.

Not young, as a rule. Most all of them sowed

their wild oats before settling down. But in the end, every last one of them took the plunge.

As a young man Alex had turned his back on the notion. He'd figured to be the exception to the rule. Besides, then the thrill of the hunt and endless variety had enticed him.

Now it often seemed more trouble than it was worth.

Sex? Well, that wasn't too much trouble. But picking up women who wanted a one-night stand seemed tawdry to him now. And while it was fine to play the field when they were young, Alex understood what every Antonides male understood—that there came a time to turn into a responsible, steady, dependable, mature man.

And that meant having a wife.

Elias might have been born responsible. But even PJ, who had been a beach bum for years, was respectably married now. In fact he had been secretly married for years. And Lukas, the youngest of them and definitely a free spirit, would get married, too.

Even Lukas knew it. It was just a matter of time.

Alex's time was now.

He had made up his mind last year. The hunt had begun to bore him and he found he preferred spending his time designing buildings than entic-

ing women into his bed. It wasn't all that difficult, honestly. The difficult part was when he had
to convince them he didn't intend to fall in love
with them.

It would be easier and more straightforward, he
decided, to find a woman he liked, spell out the
rules, marry her and get on with his life.

It wasn't as if he had a lot of rules. Basically all
he wanted was an easy-to-get-along-with, undemanding woman who wanted an easy-to-get-along-
with, undemanding husband. He wasn't looking
for love and he wasn't looking for kids. He wasn't
looking to complicate his life.

He and his wife would share bed and board when
they were in the same country and would attend
each other's duty functions when possible. Pres-
ently he lived in an apartment he'd restored in
Brooklyn above his offices, but it was a bache-
lor's pad. He wouldn't expect his wife to live there.
They could get another place close to her work.
She could choose it. He didn't care. He was perfectly willing to be accommodating.

So, really, how difficult could it be to find a
woman willing to agree to his terms?

Harder than he thought, Alex admitted now.

His last three dates had seemed promising—all
of them were professional women in their thirties.

He'd met them at business social functions. They all had high-powered careers, fast-track lives, and nearly as many demands on their time as he had on his.

They *should* have been perfect.

But the lawyer had treated their dinner date as a cross-examination about his determination not to have children. The dentist bored on about how much she hated her profession and could hardly wait to quit and start a family. And Melissa, the stock analyst with whom he'd had dinner with last night, told him point-blank that her biological clock was ticking and she wanted a baby within a year.

At least Alex had had the presence of mind to say just as firmly, "I don't."

But that date, like so many of the others he'd had since he'd decided that it was possible to marry without anything as messy as love complicating the relationship, had gone downhill from there.

Which brought him back to the receipt he held in his hand.

Daisy.

He stared at the name Lukas had scrawled on the crumpled paper. It brought with it flickers of memories, a frisson of awareness. Honey-blonde hair. Sparkling blue eyes. Laughter. Gentle, warm words. Soft sighs. Hot kisses. He shifted in the seat of the cab. Once upon a time, for one brief week-end, Alex had known a woman called Daisy.

So maybe this was fate.

The hot-kisses, soft-sighs Daisy had wanted to marry him. Maybe the matchmaking Daisy would find him a wife.

"Think of it as delegating," Elias had urged him pragmatically when he'd balked at Lukas's suggestion. "You do it all the time at work."

That was true. Alex had a whole staff at his architectural firm who did the things he didn't have time for. They did what he told them, checked availability, researched zoning and land use and materials, sorted and sifted through piles of information, then presented their findings and recommendations, and left him to make the final decision.

It was sensible. It was efficient. And Elias was right: a matchmaker could do the same thing. It would be smarter, in fact, than doing it himself.

He would be leaving less to chance if he deputized a disinterested employee to find appropriate candidates. And he'd be spared the awkwardness of future dinners like the one he'd shared with Melissa last night. With a matchmaker vetting the candidates, he would only have to meet the really suitable ones, then decide which one would make the best wife.

It suddenly sounded promising. He should have dropped in on Daisy Connolly before this. But Alex didn't ordinarily get to the Upper West Side. Today, though, he'd been working on a building project in the West Village and, finishing early, he'd had a bit of time to spare before he headed back to Brooklyn. So he'd plucked the paper out of his wallet and hopped in a cab.

Twenty minutes later he consulted it as he got out again on the corner of Amsterdam Avenue and the cross street on which Daisy Connolly had her office.

He hoped she hadn't gone home already. He hadn't made an appointment. It had seemed more sensible to leave himself the option of changing his mind if, when he saw the place, something about it made him want to walk straight on past.

But the street wore the New York City version of homey respectability. It was quiet, lined with four and five story brownstones, a few blocks north of the Museum of Natural History. The trees on either side of the street were all varying shades of gold and orange this early October afternoon, making it look like a photo op for an urban lifestyle magazine. Alex took his time walking up the block, the architect in him enjoying the view.

When he'd first bought a place to live in New York three years ago, changing his base of operations from Europe to this side of the Atlantic, he'd opted for an apartment in a high-rise about a mile south on Central Park West. Twenty-odd stories up, his aerie had given him a useful bird's-eye perspective of the city, but it had literally kept him above it all. He hadn't felt connected.

Two years ago, offered a chance to tear down a pre-war office building in Brooklyn not far from where his cousins Elias and PJ lived with their families, he'd found a purpose and a place where he was happy at the same time. He'd found another property on which to build what the owner wanted, and seeing a chance to make a useful contribution to the gentrification of a neighborhood in transition, he had snapped up the pre-war building for himself. Now he had his offices downstairs and his apartment on the fourth floor. He felt more like he belonged and less as if he were soaring above it.

He got the same feeling here on Daisy Connolly's street. There was a laundry on one corner, a restaurant on the other. Between two of the brownstones he passed an empty lot which now held a small local playground with some climbing equipment, a swing and slide. One brownstone had a small discreet plaque by the door of the garden floor apartment offering herbs and organic seedlings. Another had a small sign for a chiropractor's office.

Did matchmakers have signs? He felt an unwelcome flicker of awkwardness. When he found the address midblock, there was no sign. It looked like a version of all the rest—a tall, narrow, five story building with three stories of bay windows and another two stories above them of more modest windows—where once servants had dwelt no doubt. It was the color of warm honey, lighter than the traditional brownstone, and it sported lace curtains at the first floor bay windows making it look pleasant and professional at the same time.

Besides the lack of signs, there were no astrology signs or crystal balls in sight. No tiny fairy lights flickering in the windows, either. None of the "hocus-pocus" Lukas had mentioned. Alex breathed a sigh of relief.

He straightened his tie, took a deep breath, strode up the steps and opened the outside door. In the tiny foyer, on the mailbox for apartment 1, he saw her name: *Daisy Connolly*. Resolutely he pressed the buzzer.

For half a minute there was no response at all.

Alex shifted from one foot to the other and ground his teeth at the thought of wasting the end of an afternoon coming all the way to the Upper West Side for nothing.

But just as he was about to turn away, he heard the sound of a lock being turned. The door opened into the shadow-filled front hall and he could see the silhouette of a slim woman coming to push open the door to admit him.

She was smiling—until their gazes met. Then the smile faded and the color drained from her face.

She stared at him, stricken. "Alex?"

Honey-blonde hair. Deep blue eyes. A memory of scorching hot kisses. *"Daisy?"*

Alex? Here? No!

No. No. No.

But all the time the word was banging around inside Daisy's head, the truth—all six feet of his whipcord-lean, muscular, gorgeous male self—was staring at her in the face.

Why in heaven's name couldn't she have looked out the window before she'd answered the door?

The answer was simple: Alexandros Antonides was so far in her past she never ever considered that he might turn up on her doorstep.

She'd been expecting Philip Cannavarro.

She'd done a photo shoot with the Cannavarro family—Phil, Lottie and their three children—last month at the beach. A week and a half ago, they had chosen their photos, and Philip had called at lunch to ask if he could drop by after work and pick up their order.

So when the buzzer had sounded at twenty minutes to six, Daisy had opened the door with a smile on her face and an embossed portfolio of photos in her hand—a portfolio that the sight of Alexandros Antonides had let slip from her nerveless fingers.

"Oh, hell."

Her heart hammering, Daisy stooped quickly and began gathering up the photos. Focusing on that gave her a few moments of time and a little bit of space to get her bearings. Ha. *What was he doing here?*

She hadn't seen Alex in years and she had never expected to ever see him again. Only the fact that he seemed as surprised as she was allowed her to breathe at all.

She stopped doing that, though, when he crouched down beside her and began to help pick up the photos.

"Don't do that. Leave them," she said, trying to snatch them away from him. "I can do it!"

But Alex didn't let go. He simply kept right on. He only said, "No."

And there it was—the same single word, delivered in the same implacable tone that he'd said five years ago—that one that had pulled the rug right out from under her hopes and dreams.

Worse, though, was that his rough-edged, slightly accented, unconsciously sexy baritone still resonated all the way to the core of her exactly as it had from the moment she'd first heard him speak. It was as if he had been her very own personal pied piper of Hamelin. And foolishly, mindlessly, Daisy had fallen under his spell.

Then she'd called it "love at first sight." *Then* she had believed in the foolishness of such fairy tales.

Now she knew better. Now she knew the danger of it, thank God. There would be no falling under his spell again. She gathered the last of the photos, no longer in any shape to be presented to Philip Cannavarro, and got to her feet.

"What are you doing here?" she demanded, stepping away as he rose to his feet, too.

He shook his head, looking as dazed as she felt. "You're Daisy?" He glanced at a piece of paper he held in his hand, then frowned. "Well, of course you are, but…Connolly?"

Daisy lifted her chin. "That's right. Why?"

But before she got an answer, another man appeared outside on the stoop, just beyond the heavy front door and looked past Alex questioningly.

Daisy's knees went weak with relief. "Phil! Come on in!" He might as well have been the cavalry come to her rescue. She beamed at him.

Alex turned and stared over his shoulder, his brows drawing down. "Who's he?" he demanded as if he had more right there than her client.

Fortunately Phil was already pulling the door open, glancing in quick succession at Daisy's relieved face and Alex's scowl and finally at the photos in Daisy's hands. "Sorry. Didn't mean to interrupt—"

"You weren't," Daisy said quickly. "But I heard the bell. I thought it was you, not—" she gestured helplessly toward Alex who was standing so she could almost feel the heat of his body "—and I accidentally dropped your photos. I am so sorry." She gave Phil a hopeful smile. "I need to have them redone."

"Don't worry about it. They're probably just a little frayed at the edges," Phil said cheerfully. "No problem." He held out his hand and doubtless would have taken them from her, but Daisy shook her head and clutched them against her chest like a shield.

"No," she said. "I guarantee my work. And I don't give less than my best. You and Lottie deserve my best." He and Lottie had been one of the first matches she'd made. Lottie had been a makeup artist she'd met when she first began working as a photographer after college. Phil used to do her taxes. She felt almost like their mother even though they were older than she was. And she wasn't giving them less than her best.

"I'll put a rush on it," she promised. "You should have them in two days. I'll have them couriered directly to your house."

Phil looked doubtful. "We won't mind," he said. "Lottie will want…"

"Take these then." Daisy thrust them at him. "But tell her they're just until the new ones come in. Tell her I'm so sorry. Tell her—" She shut her mouth, the only way to stop babbling.

Phil fumbled with the photos, too, then stuffed them in his briefcase, shooting Daisy worried sidelong glances. "Are you sure you're okay?"

"I'm fine," she lied.

But she knew why he was asking. Phil and Lottie were used to the unflappable Daisy, the one who rolled with the punches, adjusted on the fly, never worried if life threw pitchforks in her path.

"Daisy always copes," Lottie said. It was like a mantra.

Daisy wasn't exactly coping now. Alex's mere presence created an electricity in the air, a force field of awareness she could never manage to be indifferent to. Damn it.

"She'll be fine," Alex said smoothly now. "She's just had a bit of a shock." He stepped even closer and looped an arm over her shoulders.

Daisy nearly jumped out of her skin. At the same time, though, her traitorous body clamored to sink into his embrace. Muscle memory was a dangerous thing. Daisy held herself rigid, resisting him, resisting her own inclination.

"She'll be all right. I'll take care of her." Alex's tone was all reassurance as he smiled and somehow put himself between her and Phil, edging the other man toward the door, making it clear that Phil didn't need to hang around.

Phil didn't hang around. He understood male territoriality as well as the next guy. "Right," he said, all smiles and cheerful bravado. "I'll tell Lottie."

And he was out the door and down the steps without glancing back.

"Thank you very much," Daisy said drily, slipping out from beneath his arm, which still managed to leave her with a sense that it was still there.

She could feel the warm weight of it even though she'd stepped away. Instinctively she wrapped her own arms across her chest.

What was he doing here? The question pounded again in her brain.

"Daisy." The way he said her name was somewhere between musing and caressing. It sent the hairs on the back of her neck straight up. A slight smile played at the corners of his mouth. "It is fate," he murmured.

"What?" Daisy said sharply.

"I was just thinking about you." His tone was warm. He acted as if they were old friends. Well, maybe to him that was all they were.

"I can't imagine why," Daisy said, which was the absolute truth.

"I'm looking for a wife."

She stared at him, her jaw dropping.

He just smiled, expecting no doubt to hear her say, *Oh, yes, please! Pick me.*

Daisy hugged her arms more tightly across her chest. "Good luck with that." She could have said, *You don't want a wife. You made a huge point of telling me you didn't want a wife!*

Now Alex raised his brows. The smile still lurking. "I wasn't proposing," he said mildly.

Mortified, Daisy said stiffly, "Of course you weren't."

She wasn't going to bring up the past at all. It did her no credit. She'd been young and stupid and far too romantic for her own good when they'd met five years ago at a wedding reception.

Daisy had been one of her college roommate, Heather's, bridesmaids, and Alex had been pressed into service as a last-minute substitute for a sick groomsman. Their eyes had met—something wild and hot and amazing had sparked between them— and to Daisy's fevered romantic twenty-three-year-old brain, it had been one of those meant-to-be moments.

They had only had eyes for each other from the moment they'd met. They talked, they danced, they laughed, they touched. The electricity between them could have lit New York City day and night for a week.

So this was love at first sight. She remembered thinking that, stunned and delighted to finally experience it. She had, of course, always believed. Her parents had always told Daisy and her sister that they'd known from the moment they'd met that they were destined to be together.

Julie, Daisy's sister, had felt that way about Brent, the moment she'd met him in eighth grade.

They'd married right out of high school. Twelve years later, they were still deeply in love.

Daisy had never felt that way—wasn't sure she believed it—until the day Alex had walked into her life.

That afternoon had been so extraordinary, so mind-numbingly, body-tinglingly perfect that she'd believed. It was just the way her parents had described it, the way Julie had described it—the sense of knowing, of a belief that all the planets were finally lined up, that the absolutely right man had come into her life.

Of course she hadn't said so. Not then. She'd just met Alex. But she hadn't wanted the day to end—and he hadn't, either. She was the bridesmaid who had been deputized to take Heather's car back to Manhattan after the reception.

"I'm coming, too," Alex had said in that rough sexy baritone, and his eyes had met hers. "If that's all right with you."

Of course it had been all right with her. It was just one more reason to believe he was feeling the same thing, too. Together they had driven back to Manhattan. And all the way there, they had talked.

He was an architect working for a multinational firm, but eager to strike out on his own. He had his own ideas, a desire to blend old and new, to create both beauty and utility and to design buildings that made people more alive, that spoke to their hearts and souls. His eyes had lit up when he'd talked about his goals, and she had shared his enthusiasm.

He had shared hers about her own professional hopes and dreams. She was working for Finn Mac-Cauley, one of the preeminent fashion and lifestyle photographers in the country. It was almost like an apprenticeship, she'd told him. She was learning so much from Finn, but was looking forward, like Alex was, to finding her own niche.

"People definitely," she'd told him. "Families, kids, people at work and play. I'd like to shoot you," she'd told him. She wanted to capture the moment, the man.

And Alex had simply said, "Whenever you want."

When they got to the city, she had left the car in the parking garage by Heather's Upper East Side apartment, then she'd taken Alex downtown on the subway to the Soho flat she was subleasing from a dental student on a semester's internship abroad.

On the subway, Alex had caught her hand in his, rubbing his thumb over her fingers, then dipping his head to touch his lips to hers. It was a light touch, the merest promise, but it set her blood on fire. And when he pulled back, she caught her breath because, looking into his eyes, she had seen a hunger there that was as deep and intense as her own.

It had never happened before. A desire so powerful, so intense just grabbed her—and it wouldn't let go. Daisy wasn't used to this sort of intensity. She didn't fall into bed at the drop of a hat, had only once before fallen into bed with a man at all. It had been fevered groping on his part and discomfort on hers.

With Alex, she'd tried telling herself, it would be more of the same.

But it wasn't.

His kisses were nothing like any she'd tasted before. They were heady, electric, bone-melting. They'd stood on the sidewalk nearly devouring each other. Not something Daisy had ever done!

She couldn't get him back to her apartment fast enough.

Once there, though, she'd felt suddenly awkward, almost shy. "Let me take your picture," she'd said.

And Alex had given her a lazy teasing smile and said, "If that's what you want."

Of course it wasn't what she wanted—or not entirely what she wanted. And it wasn't what he wanted, either. It was foreplay. Serious and smiling, goofing around, letting her direct him this way and that, all the way watching her—burning her up!—from beneath hooded lids.

He wanted her. He didn't have to say it. They circled each other, moved in, moved away. The temperature in the room rose. The temperature in Daisy's blood was close to boiling.

Then Alex had reached out and took the camera from her. He aimed, shot, posed her, caught the ferocity of her desire, as well. He stripped off his jacket, she unbuttoned his shirt. He skimmed down the zip of her dress. But before he could peel it off, she had taken the camera back, set the timer and wrapped her arms around him.

The photo of the two of them together, caught up in each other, had haunted her for years.

But at the time she hadn't been thinking about anything but the moment—the man. Within moments the camera was forgotten and in seconds more the rest of their clothing was gone.

And then there was nothing between them at all.

Alex bore her back onto her bed, settled beside her and bent his dark head, nuzzling her breasts, tasting, teasing, suckling, making her gasp and squirm.

And Daisy, shyness long gone, had been desperate to learn every inch of him. She'd prowled and played, made him suck in his breath and say raggedly, "You're killing me!"

But when she'd pulled back he'd drawn her close again. "Don't stop," he'd said.

They hadn't stopped—neither one of them. They'd driven each other to the height of ecstasy. And it wasn't at all like that other time.

With Alex there was no discomfort, there was no second-guessing, no wondering if she was doing the right thing. It had been lovemaking at its most pure and elemental, and so perfect she could have cried.

After, lying wrapped in his arms, knowing the rightness of it, she had believed completely in her mother's assertion that there was a "right man"— and about knowing instinctively when you met him.

She'd met Alex and—just like her parents, just like her sister and Brent—she had fallen in love.

They'd talked into the wee hours of the morning, sharing stories of their childhood, of their memories, of the best and worst things that had ever happened to them.

She told him about the first camera she'd ever had—that her grandfather had given her when she was seven. He told her about the first time he'd climbed a mountain and thought he could do anything. She told him about her beloved father who had died earlier that winter and about the loss she felt. He understood. He told her about losing his only brother to leukemia when he was ten and his brother thirteen. They had talked and they had touched. They had stroked and smiled and kissed.

And they had made love again. And again.

It was always going to be like that, Daisy vowed. She had met the man of her dreams, the one who understood her down to the ground, the man she would love and marry and have children with and grow old with—

—until she'd said so.

She remembered that Sunday morning as if it had been yesterday.

They'd finally fallen asleep in each other's arms at dawn. When Daisy had awakened again it was nearly ten. Alex was still asleep, sprawled on his back in her bed, bare-chested, the duvet covering him below the waist. He was so beautiful. She could have just sat there and stared at him forever, tracing the strong lines of his features, the hollows made by his collarbone, the curve of muscle in his arms, the long, tapered fingers that had made her quiver with their touch. She remembered how he'd looked, naked and primal, rising above her when they'd made love.

She would have liked to do it again. She had wanted to slide back beneath the duvet and snuggle up against him, to rub the sole of her foot up and down his calf, then let her fingers walk up and down his thigh, and press kisses to the line of dark hair that bisected his abdomen.

But as much as she wanted to do that, she also wanted to feed him before he had to catch his plane. She knew he had an early evening flight to Paris where he would be spending the next month at the main office of the firm he worked for. She'd hated the thought of him leaving, but she consoled herself by hoping that when he started his own company he would bring it stateside. Or maybe she would follow him to Paris.

Daisy had tried to imagine what living in Paris—living in Paris with Alex—would be like while she made them eggs and bacon and toast for breakfast. The thoughts made her smile. They made her toes curl.

She'd been standing at the stove, toes curling as she turned the bacon when hard muscled arms had come around her and warm breath had touched her ear.

"Morning," Alex murmured, the burr of his voice sending a shiver of longing right through her.

"Morning yourself." She'd smiled as he had

kissed her ear, her nape, her jaw, then turned her in his arms and took her mouth with a hunger that said, *The hell with breakfast. Let's go back to bed.*

But she'd fed him a piece of bacon, laughing as he'd nibbled her fingers. And she'd actually got him to eat eggs and toast as well before they'd rolled in the sheets once more.

Finally in the early afternoon he'd groaned as he sat up and swung his legs out of bed. "Got to grab a shower. Come with me?" He'd cocked his head, grinning an invitation that, despite feeling boneless already, Daisy hadn't been able to refuse.

The next half hour had been the most erotic experience of her life. Both of them had been wrung out, beyond boneless—and squeaky clean—by the time the hot water heater had begun to run cold.

"I need to go," he'd said, kissing her thoroughly once more as he pulled on a pair of cords and buttoned up his shirt.

"Yes," she agreed, kissing him back, but then turning away long enough to stuff her legs into a pair of jeans and pluck a sweater from the drawer. "I'll go out to the airport with you."

Alex had protested that it wasn't necessary, that he was perfectly capable of going off by himself, he did it all the time.

But Daisy was having none of it. She'd smiled saucily and said, "Yes, but now you have me."

She'd gone with him to the airport, had sat next to him in the back of the hired car and had shared long drugging kisses that she expected to live off until he returned.

"I'll miss you," she'd told him, nibbling his jaw. "I can't believe this has happened. That we found each other. I never really believed, but now I do."

"Believed?" Alex lifted his head from where he'd been kissing her neck long enough to gaze into her eyes. "In what?"

"This." She punctuated the word with a kiss, then looked deeply into his eyes. "You. Me. It's just like my mother said. Love at first sight." She smiled, then sighed. "I just hope we get more years than they did."

There was a sudden stillness in him. And then a slight movement as he pulled back. A small line appeared between his brows. "Years? They?"

"My parents. They fell in love like this. Took one look at each other and fell like a ton of bricks. There was never anyone else for either of them. They were two halves of the same soul. They should have had fifty years. Seventy-five," Daisy said recklessly. "Instead of twenty-six."

Alex didn't move. He barely seemed to breathe.

The sparkle in his light green eyes seemed suddenly to fade.

Daisy looked at him, concerned. "What's wrong?"

He'd swallowed. She could remember the way she'd watched his Adam's apple move in his throat, then the way he'd shaken his head slowly and said, "You're talking a lifetime, aren't you?"

And ever honest, Daisy had nodded. "Yes."

There had been a split second before the world tilted. Then Alex had sucked in a harsh breath. "No." Just the one word. Hard, decisive, determined. Then, apparently seeing the look on her face, he'd been at pains to assure her. "Oh, not for you. I'm not saying you won't have a lifetime... with someone. But...not me."

She remembered staring at him, stunned at the change in him. He seemed to have pulled inside himself. Closed off. Turned into the Ice Man as she'd watched. "What?" Even to her own ears her voice had sounded faint, disbelieving.

Alex's jaw set. "I'm not getting married," he'd told her. "Ever."

"But—"

"I don't want to."

"But—"

"No." His tone was implacable. Yet despite the

coldness of his tone, there was fire in his eyes. "No hostages to fortune," he'd said. "No wife. No kids. No falling in love. Too much pain. Never again."

"Because…because of your brother?" She had only barely understood that kind of pain. Her parents had been gloriously happily married until her father's death a month before. And she had witnessed what her mother was going through after. There was no doubt it was hard. It was hard on her and on her sister, too. But her parents had had a beautiful marriage. It had been worth the cost.

She'd tried to explain that to Alex in the car. He hadn't wanted to hear it.

"It's fine for you if that's what you want," he'd said firmly. "I don't."

"But last night…this morning…?" Daisy had been grasping desperately at straws.

"You were great," he'd said. Their gazes had met for a moment. Then deliberately Alex looked away.

By the time they'd arrived at the airport, there were no more kisses, only a silence as big and dark as the Atlantic that would soon stretch between them. Alex didn't look at her again. His fingers were fisted against his thighs as he stared resolutely out the window.

Daisy had stared at him, willed him to reconsider, to believe—to give them a chance!

"Maybe I was asking for too much too soon," she ventured at last as their hired car reached the airport departure lanes. "Maybe when you come back..."

Alex was shaking his head even as he turned and looked at her. "No," he said, his voice rough but adamant.

She blinked quickly, hoping he didn't notice the film of unshed tears in her eyes as she stared at him mutely.

"I won't be back, Daisy. A lifetime is what you want," he'd said. "I don't."

It was the last thing he'd said to her—the last time she'd seen him—until she'd opened the door a few minutes ago.

Now she dared to stare at him for just a moment as she tried to calm her galloping heart and mend her frayed nerves, tried to stuff Alexandros Antonides back into the box in the distant reaches of her mind where she'd done her best to keep him for the past five years.

It wasn't any easier to feel indifferent now than it ever had been. He was certainly every bit as gorgeous as he had been then. A shade over six feet tall, broad-shouldered in a pale blue dress shirt and a gray herringbone wool sport coat, his tie loosened at his throat, Alex looked like the consummate successful professional. His dark hair was cut a little shorter now, but it was still capable of being wind-tossed. His eyes were still that clear, light gray-green, arresting in his tanned face with its sharply defined cheekbones and blade-straight nose. And his sensuous mouth was, heaven help her, more appealing than ever with its hint of a smile.

"Why are you here?" she demanded now.

"Lukas sent me," he said.

"Lukas?"

Alex's cousin Lukas had been her official "other half" at the wedding where she'd met Alex. He'd insisted she stay by his side at the reception long enough so that his mother and aunts wouldn't fling hopeful Greek girls at his head. Once he'd established that he wasn't available, he'd given her a conspiratorial wink, a peck on the cheek and had ambled off to drink beer with his brothers and cousins, leaving her to fend for herself.

That was when she'd met Alex.

Now Alex pulled a piece of paper out of his pocket and poked it in front of her face. "He said I should talk to his friend Daisy the matchmaker."

Yes, there it was—her name, address and phone number—in Lukas's spiky handwriting. But she was more arrested by his words than what he was waving in front of her face. "You're looking for a matchmaker? *You?*"

Alex shrugged. "No doubt you're amazed," he said easily. "Thinking I've changed my mind."

She didn't know what to think.

"I haven't," he said firmly. "I'm not looking for hearts and flowers, kindred spirits, the melding of two souls any more than I ever was."

She wondered if he was being so adamant in case she decided to propose. No fear of that, she wanted to tell him. Instead she pressed her lips into a tight line.

"I want a marriage of convenience," Alex went on. "A woman with her own life, doing her own thing. She'll go her way, I'll go mine. But someone who will turn up if a business engagement calls for it. And who's there…at night."

"A sex buddy?" Daisy said drily.

Was that a line of color creeping above his shirt collar? "Friends," he said firmly. "We'll be friends. It's not just about sex."

"Hire a mistress."

"I don't want a mistress. That *is* just about sex."

"Whatever. I can't help you," she said flatly.

"Why not? You're a matchmaker."

"Yes, but I'm a matchmaker who does believe in hearts and flowers, kindred spirits, the melding of two souls." She echoed his words with a saccharine smile. "I believe in real marriages. Love matches. Soul mates. The kind you don't believe in." She met his gaze steadily, refusing to look away from those beautiful pale green eyes that she'd once hoped to drown in forever.

Alex's jaw tightened. "I believe in them," he said harshly. "I just don't want one."

"Right. So I repeat, I can't help you." She said the words again, meant them unequivocally. But even as she spoke in a calm steady tone, her heart was hammering so hard she could hear it.

Their gazes met. Locked. And with everything in her, Daisy resisted the magnetic pull that was still there. But even as she fought it, she felt the rise of desire within her, knew the feelings once more that she'd turned her back on the day he'd walked out of her life. It wasn't love, she told herself. It was something else—something as powerful and perverse and demanding as anything she'd ever felt.

But she was stronger now, and no longer an innocent. She had a life—and a love in it—that was worth resisting Alex Antonides.

"I hope you find what you're looking for," she said, holding his gaze. "It was nice to see you again."

It was, she hoped, a clear dismissal. It was also

a blatant lie. She could have gone the rest of her life without seeing Alex again and died a happy woman. She didn't need a reminder of the stupidest thirty hours of her life. But in another way, she was aware of owing him her unending gratitude.

That single day had forever changed her life.

"Was it?" he asked. His words were as speculative as his gaze. He smiled. And resist as she would, she saw in that smile the man who once upon a time had melted her bones, her resolve, every shred of her common sense, then broken her heart.

She turned away. "Goodbye, Alex."

"Daisy." His voice stopped her.

She glanced back. "What?"

The smile grew rueful, crooked, far too appealing. "Have dinner with me."

CHAPTER TWO

"WHAT? *No!*" She looked panic-stricken. Horrified.

Not at all like the Daisy he remembered. And yet she was so much the Daisy he remembered that Alex couldn't just turn and walk away. Not now. Not when he'd finally found her again. "Why not?"

"Because…because I don't want to!" Her cheeks had grown red in the throes of passion. Her whole body had blushed when he'd made love to her. His body—right now—was already contemplating doing the same thing again.

Which was a profoundly stupid idea, considering what he wanted, what she wanted, considering the present—and their past.

"Do you hate me?" he asked. He remembered the way they had parted. She'd looked devastated, about to cry. Thank God she hadn't. But what she'd wanted—the hope of a lifetime of love—was his worst nightmare. It brought back memories that he'd turned his back on years ago. What had begun happening between them that weekend was something he wasn't ready for. Would never be ready for.

So there was no point in making her hope in vain. He regretted having hurt her when he'd left her. But he could never bring himself to regret that weekend. It was one of the best memories of his life.

"Of course I don't hate you," she said briskly now. "I don't care at all about you."

Her words were a slap in the face. But he supposed he had it coming. And it was just as well, wasn't it, that she didn't care? It meant he hadn't hurt her badly after all.

"Well, then," he suggested easily, "let's share a meal." He gave her his best engaging grin. "For old times' sake," he added when he could see the word *no* forming on her lips.

"We don't have old times."

"We have one old time," he reminded her softly.

Her cheeks grew brighter yet. "That was a long, long time ago. Years. Five or six at least."

"Five," he said. "And a half." He remembered clearly. It was right after that weekend that he'd made up his mind to stay in Europe, to buy a place in Paris.

It made sense businesswise, he'd told himself

at the time. But it wasn't only business that had made him dig in across the pond. It was smarter to put an ocean between himself and the temptation that was Daisy.

She was still tempting. But a dinner he could handle. "It's just a meal, Daisy. I promise I won't sweep you off to bed." Not that he wouldn't like to.

"You couldn't," she said flatly.

He thought he could, but emotions would get involved. So he wouldn't go there, as tempting as it was. Still, he wasn't willing to walk away, either. "We have a lot to catch up on," he cajoled.

But Daisy shook her head. "I don't think so." Her smile was brittle. He saw none of the sunny sincerity he'd always associated with his memories of her. Interesting.

He studied her now, wondering what her life had been like over the past five years. He'd always imagined she'd found the true love she'd been seeking, had found a man who'd made her happy. And if the thought occasionally had made him grind his teeth, he told himself a guy couldn't have everything. He had what he wanted.

Now he wondered if Daisy had got what she wanted. Suddenly he wanted to know.

"Another time then," he suggested.

"Thank you, but no."

He knew he was going to get "no" if he asked a hundred times. And the knowledge annoyed him. "Once upon a time we had a lot to say to each other," he reminded her.

"Once upon a time is for fairy tales, Alex. Now, if you'll excuse me, I have to go."

"Let's," he said readily. "I'll walk with you."

"I don't mean go somewhere else," she said. "I mean I have to go back inside. I have work to do. In my office."

"Matchmaking?"

She shook her head. "Not tonight."

"Photography?" He remembered the camera, how it had been almost a natural extension of who she was.

She nodded, smiling a little. It was a real smile.

"You've got your own business then?" he pressed.

"Yes." She nodded. The smile stayed.

"Families? Kids? People of all shapes and sizes?" And at her further nod, he said, "Show me."

She almost moved toward the door, almost started to invite him in. But then she stayed where she was, gave her head a little shake. "I don't think so."

"You took photos of us." Sometimes he'd wished he had one. To take out and remember. But that was stupid. It was better to forget.

She shrugged and looked just a little uncomfortable. He wondered if she still had the photos.

"Why matchmaking?" he asked her suddenly.

She shrugged. "Long story." And no invitation to ask her to tell it.

He lifted a corner of his mouth. "I've got time."

"I don't."

"You're scared."

The color in her cheeks bloomed again. "I am not scared! What's there to be scared of?"

"I don't know. You tell me." He cocked his head. "Temptation maybe?"

She shook her head adamantly. "I'm not tempted. I'm busy. I have things to do. I haven't seen you in five years, Alex. I barely knew you then. We don't have a past to catch up on."

"We had a hell of a lot." He didn't know why he was persisting, but he couldn't seem to leave it alone.

"And we wanted to do different things with it. Goodbye, Alex." She turned away and started to go back inside.

But before she could, Alex caught her arm, and spun her slowly back, then did what he'd been wanting to do ever since he'd realized who she was.

He dipped his head and kissed her.

It was instinct, desire, a mad impetuous hunger that he couldn't seem to control. It was a roaring in his ears and a fire in his veins. It was the taste of Daisy—a taste he'd never forgotten. *Never.* And as soon as he tasted her, he wanted more.

And more.

For a second, maybe two, Daisy seemed to melt under the touch of his lips. She went soft and pliable, shaping her mouth to his. And then, in another instant, it was over.

She jerked away from him, stared at him for one horrified moment, cheeks scarlet, mouth still forming an astonished O. Then she pulled out of his grasp and bolted back inside the foyer.

"Daisy!"

The door slammed in his face.

Alex stared after her, still tasting her. Jolted, intrigued, stunned. Aroused.

Five years ago Daisy had been like a siren he'd followed eagerly, mindlessly, hungrily. He'd wanted her on every level imaginable. And having her that weekend over and over hadn't assuaged his hunger. He'd only wanted more.

Leaving, thank God, had removed the temptation.

And now—within minutes of having seen her again—it was back. In spades.

It was the last thing he wanted. The last thing he needed.

Alex turned and walked down the steps, pausing only to drop the paper with her name and address in the trash.

She had been right to say no. He would be smart and walk away.

Ten minutes later Daisy was still shaking.

She sat at her desk, staring at the photo she was editing, and didn't see it at all. Eyes closed or open, she only saw Alex—older, harder, stronger, handsomer—in every way *more*, even more compelling than the younger Alex had been.

She shuddered and scrubbed at her mouth with her fingers, trying to wipe away the taste of his kiss.

But all the scrubbing in the world wouldn't do that, and she knew it. She'd tried to forget it for years. It hadn't done a whit of good.

She hadn't even tried to forget him. That would have been impossible. But as time passed, at least she'd managed to put him on a shelf in the back of her memory's closet. He was still there, but he couldn't hurt her.

But now Alex was here.

She'd just seen him, talked to him. Been kissed

by him. Had almost, heaven help her, kissed him back. It had felt so right, so perfect, so exactly the way it had felt the first time.

But she knew better now.

He had come. He had gone. The other shoe had finally dropped. He wouldn't come back.

"And it wouldn't matter if he did," Daisy said aloud.

Because if one thing was completely obvious, it was that however much more he had become, in fundamentals, Alex hadn't changed a bit.

He might want to get married now, but he obviously didn't want anything more than "friends— with benefits." He didn't want love. He didn't want a real marriage. He didn't want a family.

He didn't want her.

For a nanosecond her traitorous heart had dared to believe he'd finally come to his senses, had learned the value of love, of relationships, of life- time commitment.

Thank goodness, a nanosecond was all the time it had taken her to realize that there was no point in getting her hopes up.

Of course he had proved he still wanted her on one level—the one he had always wanted her on. She wasn't such an innocent that she didn't know desire when she felt it. And she had felt it hard and firm against her when Alex had kissed her and pressed his body against hers.

But physical desire was just that—a basic instinctive response. It had nothing to do with things that really mattered—love, commitment, responsibility, sharing of hearts and souls, dreams and desires.

It was nothing more than an itch to be scratched.

And she wasn't about to be a matchmaker for a pairing like that. If he was interested in nothing more than a woman to share his bed—but not his heart—he wouldn't be interested in the sort of marriages she believed in. So he wouldn't be back.

And thank God for that—because if her heart still beat faster at the very sight of him and her body melted under his touch, at least her mind knew he was the last person she needed in her life.

Not just in her life, but in the life of the person she loved most in all the world—the one who, at this very moment, she could hear pounding his way up the stairs from the kitchen.

"Mom!" His voice was distant at first, then louder. "Mom!" And louder still as the door banged open. "Mom! Aren'tcha finished working yet? It's time to go."

Charlie.

Four and three-quarter years of sunshine and

skinned knees and wet kisses and impatience all rolled up in the most wonderful person she knew.

He skidded to a stop in front of her and looked up at her, importuning. "Mom!"

"Charlie!" She smiled at him, echoing his tone, loving him with all her heart.

"Are you ready?" he demanded.

"Almost." She turned back to close the file she hadn't done a thing to since Alex had shown up on the doorstep. "Almost," she repeated, taking a deep breath to steady her nerves, then shutting the file.

She wished she could shut her memories of Alex down as easily. She couldn't. Particularly she couldn't right now—faced with the small boy staring up at her, all quivering impatience.

Impatience wasn't Charlie's middle name, but maybe it should have been. He'd been eager and energetic since the moment of his birth. Before his birth, in fact. He'd come almost two weeks early, right before Christmas. And he'd been taking the world by storm ever since.

He had a chipped tooth from a fall out of a tree back in May. He had a scab on his knee beneath his jeans even now. Daisy had told him last week she was going to buy stock in the Band-Aid company, and after he'd wrinkled his nose and said,

"What's stock?" he'd listened to her brief explanation and said, "Good idea."

His stick-straight hair, the color of honey shot through with gold, was very close to the same shade as her own. But his light eyes were nothing like her stormy dark blue.

He didn't look like Alex—except for the shape of his eyes.

And after nearly five years, she was inured to it. She didn't see Alex in him every time she looked at him. She saw Charlie himself—not Alex's son.

Except today. Today the eyes were Alex's. The impatience was Alex's. The "let's get moving" was Alex down to the ground.

"In good time," she said now, determined to slow Charlie down—a little, at least. But she managed a smile as she shut the computer down. And she was sure she was the only one who noticed her hands were shaking.

"You said we'd go at six-thirty. It's almost six-thirty. The game's gonna start." He grabbed one of Daisy's hands and began to tug her back toward the stairs.

"Coming," Daisy said. But she straightened her desk, made a note to reorder the Cannavarro files, put her pencil in the drawer. All very methodical. Orderly. Step by step. Pay attention to detail. From the day that she'd learned she was pregnant, it was how she'd managed to cope.

Charlie bounced from one foot to the other until she finished and finally held out a hand to him again. "Okay. Let's go." She allowed herself to be towed down the stairs.

"We gotta hurry. We're gonna be late. Come on. Dad's pitching."

Dad. One more reason she prayed that Alexandros Antonides didn't darken her door again.

"Hey, Sport." Cal dropped down beside Charlie on the other side of the blanket that Daisy had spread out to sit on while they watched the softball game.

They had been late, as Charlie feared, arriving between innings. But at least Cal, Daisy's ex-husband, had already pitched in his half, so he could come sit with them until it was his turn to bat.

"We made a fire engine," Charlie told him. "Me 'n' Jess. Outta big red cardboard blocks—this big!" He stretched his hands out a couple of feet at least.

Cal looked suitably impressed. "At preschool?"

Charlie bobbed his head. "You an' me could make one."

"Okay. On Saturday," Cal agreed. "But we'll have to use a cardboard box and paint it red. Grandpa will be in town. I'll tell him to bring paint."

Charlie's eyes got big. "Super! Wait'll I tell Jess 'bout ours."

"You don't want to make him jealous," Cal warned. He grinned at Charlie, then over the boy's head at his mother.

Daisy smiled back and told herself that nothing had changed. Nothing. She and Charlie were doing what they often did—dropping by to watch Cal play ball in Central Park, which he and a few diehards continued to do well after the softball leagues ended in the summer. Now, in early October, there was a nip in the air, and the daylight was already going. But they continued to play.

And she and Charlie would continue to come and watch.

It was the joy of a civilized divorce, Daisy often reminded herself. She and Cal didn't hate each other—and they both loved Charlie.

"—you?"

She realized suddenly that Cal was no longer talking to Charlie. He was talking to her. "Sorry," she said, flustered. "I was just…thinking about something."

"Apparently," Cal said drily. Then he looked at her more closely. "What's wrong?"

"Nothing." She looked around. "Where's Charlie?"

Cal nodded in the direction of the trees where

Charlie and the son of another one of the players were playing in the dirt. "He's fine. You're not. Something's wrong."

"No. Why should anything be wrong?" That was the trouble with Cal. He'd always been able to read her like a book.

"You're edgy. Distracted. Late," he said pointedly.

"I didn't realize you were timing me. I've got things on my mind, Cal. Work—"

But he cut her off. "And you're biting my head off, which isn't like you, Daze. And you must've come on the bus."

"The bus?" she said stupidly.

"You always walk, so Charlie can ride his bike." Cal looked around pointedly. There was no bike because, he was right, they hadn't had time to bring it. Charlie wanted to ride his bike everywhere. It was the smallest two-wheeler Daisy had ever seen, but Charlie loved it. Daisy was sure he would have slept with it every night if she hadn't put her foot down. Cal had given it to Charlie for his fourth birthday.

Daisy had protested, had said he was too young, that no four-year-old needed a bike.

"Not every four-year-old," Cal had agreed. "Just this one." He'd met her skeptical gaze with confident brown eyes and quiet certainty. "Because he wants it more than anything on earth."

Daisy couldn't argue with that. If Charlie's first word hadn't been *bike* it had been in the first ten. He'd pointed and crowed, "Bike!" well before his first birthday. And he'd been desperate for a bicycle last winter. She hadn't thought it would last. But Cal had insisted, and he'd been right.

Charlie's eyes had shone when he'd spotted the bike that morning. And over the past six months, his love for it had only grown. Since Cal had helped him learn to balance and he could now ride it unaided, Charlie wanted to ride it everywhere.

Usually she let him ride to the park while she walked alongside him. But they had been late today because…because of her visitor.

She was suddenly aware that Cal was watching her, not the game. "He doesn't have to ride his bike every time," she said testily. "And it's nearly dark."

"True." Cal stretched his legs out in front of him and leaned back, resting his weight on his elbows and forearms as his gaze slowly moved away from her to focus on the game, yelling at the batter to focus. Then, still keeping his gaze on the batter, he persisted quietly, "So why don't you just tell me."

He wasn't going to leave it alone. She'd never won an argument with Cal. She'd never been able to convince him of anything. If he was wrong, he couldn't be told. He always had to figure it out himself—like his "I can love anyone I will myself to" edict. He'd been as wrong about that as she had been about her "love at first sight" belief.

Clearly, when it came to love, the two of them didn't know what they were talking about.

Now he stared at her and she plucked at the grass beside the blanket, stared at it. *Nothing's changed. Nothing's changed.* She tried to make it into a mantra so she could convince herself. But she was no better at lying to herself than she was at lying to her ex-husband. Finally she raised her gaze to meet his as he turned away from the game to look at her. "I saw Alex."

There was the crack of bat hitting ball. Whoops and yells abounded.

Cal never turned his head to see what happened. His eyes never left Daisy's. He blinked once. That was all. The rest of his body went still, though. And his words, when they came, were quiet. "Saw him where?"

Daisy ran her tongue over dry lips. "He came to my office."

Cal waited, not pressing, allowing her to tell the story in her own way, in her own time.

And she couldn't quite suppress the ghost of a

smile that touched her lips. "Looking for a match-maker."

"What!" Cal's jaw dropped.

Hysterical laughter bubbled up just as it had threatened to do when Alex told her. This time Daisy gave in to it. "He's looking for a wife."

"You?" Cal demanded.

"No. He was as surprised as I was when he knocked on my door. He didn't know he was coming to see me."

"Then how—?"

"Lukas sent him."

Cal's eyes widened. His teeth came together. "Lukas needs to mind his own business."

"Of course. But Lukas never does. Besides, he didn't have any idea what he was doing. He never knew about Alex and me. No one did." No one ever had except Cal—and only because when she'd discovered she was pregnant, she'd had to talk to someone. "Don't blame Lukas. He thinks he's doing me a favor sending clients my way. And he is, I suppose. Most of the time. Not this time," she said quietly.

"No." Cal stared down at his fingers plucking at the grass for a moment. Then his gaze lifted and went toward Charlie who was still playing with his friend in the dirt. The question was there, but unspoken.

"I didn't say a word."

"But he—"

Daisy shook her head. "No. That hasn't changed. He wouldn't want to know."

"Still?" Cal persisted.

"No. He doesn't want relationships any more than he ever did," Daisy said firmly. "He doesn't want a real wife—he wants a woman to take to social events and go to bed with. It will save him the effort of having to go out and find one, charm one."

"He charmed you," Cal pointed out.

Cal, of course, knew that. He knew the whole sordid story.

She had met Cal Connolly when she'd taken the job with Finn after college. Cal had been the photographer she'd replaced, Finn's assistant before her.

Even after Cal hung out his own shingle, he had regularly come by Finn's to talk shop. Daisy had been included in the conversation. She learned a great deal from both of them.

Finn was brilliant, mercurial—and impatient. Cal was steadier, calmer, more methodical. He didn't yell quite as much. Finn had a wife and growing family. Cal was single, on his own. So it was Cal she began to spend time with. And while Finn had always remained her mentor, Cal had quickly become her best pal.

When she wasn't working for Finn, she had spent hours working with Cal, talking with him, arguing with him. They argued about everything from camera lenses to baseball teams to sushi rolls, from free will to evolution to love at first sight.

That had always been their biggest argument: did you love because—bang!—it hit you between the eyes? Or did you love because you decided who the right person was and made up your mind?

Because of her parents, Daisy had been a staunch believer in the "love at first sight" notion.

"I just haven't met the right person," she had maintained over and over. "When I do, I'll know. In an instant. And it will be perfect."

But Cal had scoffed at that. Ever the logical realist, he'd said, "Nonsense. I don't believe it for a minute. That makes you nothing but a victim of your hormones."

"It's not hormones. It's instinct."

But Cal had disagreed. "You can will whom you love," he'd told her firmly. "It's a rational decision."

So when he'd proposed to her, he'd been determined to demonstrate just that. "Obviously your way doesn't work," he'd pointed out. "So we'll try it my way now."

And Daisy, because she did love Cal—just not the way she thought she loved Alex—had faced the truth of her own folly. And she'd said yes.

It turned out they were both wrong. But they'd given it their best shot. And Daisy still did believe in love—now she had a codicil: it was apparently for other people.

Now Daisy let out a sigh and wrapped a blade of grass around her finger where Cal's wedding ring once had been.

"So, are you going to do it? Matchmake for him?" Cal asked.

"Of course not."

He grunted. "Good." He stared out across the field. "Was it...the same? Did you feel...this time... what you felt before?"

It was all Daisy could do not to touch her tongue to her lips. Instead she pulled her knees up and wrapped her arms around them, in full cocoon mode. "He's still charming," she admitted.

Cal had been watching the next batter swing and miss. But at her words he turned his head and shot her a sharp glance.

Daisy gave him a quick humorless smile. "Speaking objectively. Don't worry. I'm not a fool any-more."

"So I should hope."

The batter swung and missed. Cal hauled him-self to his feet to go pitch another inning. "You all right? Anything I can do?"

"No. He won't be back."

Cal cocked his head. "No?" He didn't sound so sure.

"Why would he? I didn't invite him in. I didn't encourage him at all." *I didn't kiss him back!* "And he doesn't want me. He wants some woman who won't care."

"And Charlie?"

"He doesn't know about Charlie. I'm doing him a favor, really," she said firmly. "He doesn't want kids. He never did."

"Because he doesn't think he has any," Cal pointed out. "What if he finds out he does?"

"He won't."

"But if—" Cal persisted. It was what she hated about him.

"Charlie is mine! And yours."

She had always told Charlie—not that he under-stood yet really—that he had two fathers—a birth father who had given him life, and Cal, the father he knew. Charlie didn't question it. Someday he would, no doubt. But by then it would be ingrained in his mind. There would never be a time when she had to "tell him" his father was not Cal.

Because in every way that counted, his father was Cal. Cal was the one who had been there for her. He'd been her husband when Charlie was born. Charlie bore his surname. He was the only father Charlie knew.

If someday he wanted to know about Alex, she'd tell him. If someday in the distant future, Alex learned he had a child, perhaps they would meet. But not now. Now Charlie was a child. He was vulnerable. He didn't need a father who didn't want him.

"You don't know what he'll do, Daze," Cal said heavily, "if he finds out."

"He won't find out." She would make sure of that.

Cal's smile was grim. "We hope."

CHAPTER THREE

A DAY went by. Two.

Daisy still kept looking over her shoulder—well, out the window, actually—feeling skittish. Apprehensive.

She checked the caller ID every time the phone rang. Her breath caught whenever she saw a shadow on the front steps.

She actually dropped the kettle she was filling this morning, even though it was just the FedEx man bringing an order to Mrs. Kaminski upstairs.

Now she was filling it again for her friend Nell, who had just brought Charlie home from preschool and was staying for a cup of tea and regarding her curiously all the while.

"Something wrong?"

"No. I just…dropped the kettle this morning. I'm trying to be more careful now." Daisy set it on the burner and turned the gas on.

"Cal giving you trouble?" It was always the first thing Nell thought of because her own ex-husband, Scott, was a continual source of irritation.

"Cal never gives me trouble," Daisy said. She glanced out the sliding door to the garden where Charlie and Nell's son Geoff were playing with trucks.

Nell grimaced. "Lucky you. Scott's driving me crazy."

Daisy wasn't glad to hear that Scott was creating difficulties in her friend's life, but talking about it did avert Nell's further interest in Daisy's edginess. She gave Daisy an earful about her ex while they drank their tea and ate biscotti. Daisy made soothing sounds, but Nell was still grumbling when she decided it was time to go. She called Geoff in and they headed out the front door.

Relieved that her life was nowhere near as complicated as her friend's, Daisy was feeling much more sanguine when the phone rang as the door shut behind Nell and her son.

"Daisy Connolly," she said brightly into the phone.

"Daisy." The voice was warm, slightly gruff and instantly recognizable. The intimate tone of it made the hairs on the back of Daisy's neck stand straight up. Why hadn't she checked the ID this time?

"Yes. This is Daisy," she said crisply. "Who is this?"

"You know who it is." There was a smile in his voice as he called her bluff.

"Alex," she said flatly because playing the fool any longer wasn't going to help matters a bit.

"See. I knew you'd figure it out." He was grinning now. She could hear that, too.

"What do you want?"

"Are you married?"

"What?"

"I remembered you weren't Daisy Connolly back then. Wasn't your last name Harris? Morris?"

"Harris."

There was a brief silence. "So you did marry." It wasn't a question.

"Yes," she said firmly.

"And now?"

"What do you mean, and now?" Why did he have to ask? What business was it of his?

"Are you still…married?"

What kind of question was that? Damn it. She wanted to lie. But she'd never been a good liar, and though her acquaintance with Alex hadn't been long, it had been intense. She was sure he would be able to tell if she did.

"I'm divorced." She bit the words out.

"Ah."

Which meant what? Never mind. She didn't want

to know. "Alex," she said with all the patience she could muster. "I'm working."

"This is work."

"No. I told you, I'm not matchmaking for you."

"I got that. You don't want what I want." He parroted her sentiments back to her. "This is photography. Or are you going to turn me down for that, too?"

She opened her mouth, wanting desperately to do exactly that. But she wouldn't give him the satisfaction of knowing he'd rattled her. "What sort of photography?" she said. "I do family stuff."

"And weddings. And bar mitzvahs. And some professional head shots. Some editorial. Recreation. Ice skating," he added. "Frisbee in the park. Baseball games." He ticked off half a dozen scenarios that were all shoots she had actually done.

"How do you know that?"

"You have a website," he reminded her. "The internet is a wonderful thing."

Daisy, grinding her teeth, wasn't so sure. Her fingers tapped an irritated staccato on the countertop. Outside Charlie was making vrooming noises as he pushed his cars around the patio. Any minute he'd slide open the door and want a snack. To prevent it, she latched the sliding door and got some crackers out of the cupboard and cheese from the refrigerator, preempting his demand. "What did you have in mind?" she asked.

"I need photos. An architectural journal is doing a piece on me and some of the work I've done. They've got photos of my projects from all over the world. Now they want some of me on one of the sites." He paused. "They said they could send a photographer—"

"Then let them."

"But I'd rather have you."

She wanted to say, Why? But she didn't want to hear his answer. Besides, asking would open a whole new can of worms.

"Not my line," she said briskly as she slapped cheese between the crackers and made little sandwiches for Charlie.

"You do editorial. I've seen magazine articles."

"Yes. But I don't traipse all over the world. I work in the city."

"The building is in Brooklyn." He gave her a second to digest that, then added, "I seem to remember you cross the river."

They had crossed the river together coming back from the wedding on Long Island. Daisy felt the walls closing in.

"Yes, I cross the river. *If* I have time. I'm busy."

"Any time in the next two weeks," he said

smoothly. "And don't tell me that every minute of your life is booked."

Daisy heard the challenge in his voice. It was just another way of saying, *I don't believe you're really over me at all. You still want me. And now that you're divorced you might not believe in that ridiculous "love at first sight" notion anymore. You might be glad for a roll in bed.*

And, if it weren't for Charlie, heaven help her, she might.

"Are you still there? Daisy?" he prompted when she didn't reply.

She drew a breath. "I might have something next week. Let me check." It was the only way she could think of to prove to him—and to herself—that she wasn't a weak-willed fool.

She put the cracker sandwiches on a paper plate, flipped up the latch and slid open the door. Charlie looked up and, at the sight of the plate, grinned and jumped to his feet.

Daisy put a finger to her lips to shush him before he could speak, grateful that she'd taught him almost since he could talk not to blurt things out where people on the phone could hear him. That way, she'd explained, he wouldn't have to have a babysitter as often if she could take calls as if she were in her office when, in fact, she was at home.

Charlie had learned quickly. Now he stuffed a cracker sandwich into his mouth, then carried the plate back to his trucks. For a moment, Daisy just watched him and felt her heart squeeze with love. Then quietly she slid the door shut and went to look at her appointment book.

"Where in Brooklyn? What sort of photos?" she asked as she flipped through the pages of her day planner.

"Park Slope." Alex gave her the address. "It's a pre-war building."

"I thought you were an architect. Don't you design new buildings?"

"Not this one. I built this one from the inside out. The outside is pretty much intact, except for the windows. I fixed the windows. The place was in really awful shape and the guy who owned it wanted it removed. He wanted me to put up a new building there. But when I got into it, I couldn't see tearing it down. Structurally it was sound. And it had some really strong period architectural features. It fit the block, the surroundings. So I made him a deal. I bought it from him and he bought land a couple of miles away. Then I built him what he wanted there, and I kept this one for myself."

The eagerness and the satisfaction in his voice reminded her of when he'd talked about his hopes for his career. He'd already done some big projects for the company he'd worked for then. But those had been projects he'd been assigned, ones that had been the vision of someone else. Now it sounded like he had taken the reins and was making his own choices, his own decisions.

"Are you your own boss now?" she asked, unable not to.

"For the last five years." He hesitated, then went on so smoothly she might have imagined the brief pause. "There was never going to be the perfect time to leave, so I just… jumped in."

"You like it?"

"Couldn't be happier," he said. "What about you? You've obviously left the guy you were working for."

"Finn? Yes. And I like what I'm doing, too."

"You can tell me all about it—if you can see a way to work me into your schedule?"

He made it sound very straightforward. A job. No more. No less. Maybe this really was all business.

Daisy could almost—but not quite—forget the way he'd kissed her. Deliberately she shoved the thought away. "What sort of thing does the writer have in mind?" she asked. "What do they want to feature?"

"Me," Alex said ruefully. "Up-and-coming archi-

tect, blah, blah, blah. I designed a hospital wing—
first one I've done—and it's up for some award."

"That's great." And not surprising, really. She
imagined that Alex would be good at whatever he
did. "Where? Nearby?"

"Upstate a ways. Same side of the river, though,"
he added drily. "They used staff photos for that.
They want ones of me and of the place in Brooklyn because it's a new departure for me. So you'd
be shooting it now—plenty of awful 'then' photos
already available. And then they want some of me
'in my environment.'" His tone twisted the words
wryly. "With a pencil protector in my pocket."
She could hear his grin. "Playing with blueprints.
I don't know. You will."

If she did it. And maybe she should. Maybe it
was exactly what she needed to do—learn about
the man, demythologize him, turn him into some
digital files and eight-by-ten-inch glossies.

"I can spare a bit of time next Thursday afternoon. Say, around three?"

"Great. I'll pick you up."

"I'll meet you. Just give me the address again."
It was business. Just business.

He gave her the address. She wrote it down.

Then he said, "See you Thursday. Bye."

And he was gone. Just like that.

* * *

She had second thoughts. And third. And thirty-third. By the time Saturday rolled around, it was all she could think about.

"So call him and tell him you can't," Cal said when he came by to pick up Charlie Saturday morning. Charlie had already given her a smacking kiss goodbye and bolted out the door eager to tell his grandfather about the fire engine they were going to make.

But Cal hadn't followed him. He was eying her curiously as Daisy told him about Alex's call and his offer of the photography job. She also admitted to her qualms.

"It's just…distracting!" She stuck her hands in her hair and tugged.

"Why do it then? Call him up and tell him no."

"He'll want to know why."

"You're not obliged to tell him."

"If I don't, he'll get suspicious."

"About what? Is he going to think you're hiding his son from him?"

"No, of course not. He'll think—" Daisy hesitated "—that I'm still in love with him. That I don't trust myself around him."

"Possible," Cal agreed. "Or maybe you don't trust him."

Maybe she didn't trust either of them. The attraction was still there on a physical level. She hadn't told Cal about Alex's kiss. Or her reaction to it. There were some things better left unsaid. Now she just shrugged. "It'll be all right," she murmured.

Cal gave her a long hard look. She tried to remain indifferent under his gaze, but Cal was a photographer, too. He saw things that other people couldn't see.

"Is it just hormones?" he said at last. "Or something more?"

Daisy flushed, giving him yet another telltale sign. "I'm curious about what he's done with the building. About the sort of work he's doing."

"Uh-huh." Cal wasn't having any of it.

"Really. I wouldn't jeopardize Charlie's future. You know that." She looked at him steadily.

"Keep it in mind," Cal warned.

"No fear. I'm not an airy-fairy fool anymore."

Cal looked as if he doubted that. But at last he shrugged. "If you say so."

"In fact," Daisy added, "I think this may be a good thing. I can learn more about his real life, so I'll be able to tell Charlie about it someday."

"Oh, there's a plus," Cal muttered.

"It'll be fine." She put a hand on his sleeve. "Really, Cal. Don't worry."

Cal let out a slow breath. "I'm trying not to." He started toward the door and then turned back. "Charlie hasn't seen him? He hasn't seen Charlie?"

"No!" She smiled her best reassuring smile.

"Someday..."

"Someday they'll meet. Someday when Charlie is older. Grown-up. Settled. And if he has questions in the meantime, I'll answer them. But I'm not setting him up to be hurt! You know that. We've discussed it." When a man felt about having kids the way Alex did, deliberately introducing him into Charlie's life wasn't a risk she wanted to take.

Besides, he had a perfectly fine father in Cal. And one father was enough—for the moment at least.

"C'mon, Dad!" Charlie poked his head out of the window of the car.

"Go on, Dad," Daisy urged him. "And don't you worry. I'm doing enough for both of us. And it's silly, really. I will be fine. I'll shoot his photos, admire his handsome face and come home. End of story. Trust me. I can take care of myself."

The building Alex had restored wasn't far from Prospect Park. Daisy found it easily. It sat on the corner of a residential street filled with brownstones and trees and a business cross street that was wider, had fewer trees to block the view, and gave her plenty of scope.

She'd arrived early to scope out the neighborhood, wanted to get herself in work-mode before she ever laid eyes on him. The day was cool and crisp, the trees in their full autumn glory as she walked down the block, studying the building side on.

At a few minutes before three the sun was low enough that the shadows picked out some of the ornate carved relief on the facing of the top floor, sharpening the detail, showing the building to best advantage. Daisy took out her camera before she was halfway down the block, framed and shot. She took a dozen or more, then crossed the main thoroughfare to study the angles.

The building was tall and narrow, a four story redbrick like others in the neighborhood, but, unlike the rest of them, it seemed somehow to draw in the light.

She studied it more closely, trying to understand what she was seeing. The ground floor housed an electronics store which seemed an odd tenant for an old building. But somehow it fit the space easily and looked as if it belonged. Studying it, she began to realize why. The windows were taller than those in other buildings on the block and she remembered Alex saying he had changed the windows. But they still fit the period; they belonged. But he'd made the proportions just that little bit more generous.

Now they fit twenty-first century people. It made all the difference.

The second floor echoed the look with a series of gothic-arched windows and cream-colored facings that contrasted with the dark red brick. Stenciled just above waist height across the central largest window in black sans serif was Antonides Architectural Design. Simple, spare, elegant.

She could see possibilities forming as she moved quickly along the sidewalk. She would shoot Alex standing in that window, looking out, master of his kingdom. And another at his drafting table. She could envision him in her mind's eye bending over a drawing, black hair drifting across his forehead as he studied his work intently.

There would doubtless be plenty of other possibilities inside; an open staircase perhaps or a period elevator or maybe a skylight and, she grinned delightedly—enough light to make it happen.

Suddenly enthused and feeling like a real competent professional photographer for the first time since Alex had asked her to do it, Daisy turned— and came up hard against a solid male chest.

CHAPTER FOUR

"I SAW you wandering back and forth across the street. I thought you might be lost." Alex had caught hold of her when she'd turned and crashed into him. He was still holding on now. Their bodies were touching.

Daisy's heart was going a mile a minute. Hastily she pulled away from his hard chest. "I wasn't lost," she said, hating her sudden breathlessness. "I was studying the building. Looking at all the angles."

She squinted up at him, trying not to be bowled over by the casual magnetism of the man. What was it about Alexandros Antonides that drew her like a moth to a flame?

Well, he was still gorgeous, there was that. Tall, whip-cord lean, broad-shouldered. Masculinity defined. Alex didn't have to flaunt the testosterone. It wasn't a veneer he put on. It was clearly bedrock in him.

"Well, if you're done assessing all the angles, let

me show you around." He gave her one of those smiles, too, the one that had, from the beginning, undermined her common sense.

But she was older now, Daisy reminded herself. Made of sterner stuff. And she knew what he was made of, too.

"Fine," she said briskly. "Lead on."

He did just that, but not before he plucked her camera bag and one of the tripods out of her hands, leaving her with only her purse and the smaller tripod. "You could have left that in the building while you were looking around," he said over his shoulder as he crossed the street.

"I suppose."

"How'd you get here?"

"Subway."

He turned as he stepped up onto the sidewalk in front of his building. "With all this stuff? For God's sake, Daisy! They have cabs in Manhattan!"

"It's more efficient to take the subway."

"I'd have paid the cab fare."

"I don't need your cab fare. It's a business expense. When I want to take a taxi, I take one. I prefer the subway when I'm coming to Brooklyn. No bridge tie-ups. Now can we get going?"

She didn't want him fussing over her. He had no

right. She didn't need him—of all people—thinking he knew best what was good for her.

Alex grunted, but still he shook his head as if despairing of her as he pushed open the door to the building. The electronics store she'd already spotted had its entrance off this interior vestibule on one side of the building. On the other was a stationer's shop—all fine paper and cards and pens.

"The old and the new," Daisy remarked, looking from the stationer's to the electronics store, nodding. She'd work that in, too.

Meanwhile he was leading her into the electronics store, pointing out the new windows and the old oak paneling, the new built-in oak cabinets and the old tin ceilings now restored. It was an artful blend of the best of both, and it showed off the latest electronic devices spectacularly well. After a quick tour there, he took her into the stationer's shop, and the same was true there, as well.

The exquisite paper products looked appealing against the same oak cabinetry. The displays of calligraphic pens and multicolored inks and artists' tools were equally appealing.

Against the tall narrow windows Alex had created window seats which the proprietor had set up as inviting nooks for one or two people to sit and try out the various products. They were all full—and many of the customers were as young and hip as those in the electronics store across the vestibule.

"I'll show you photos of how it was before when we go upstairs," he said. "In the meantime, shoot whatever you want. Den and Caroline—the owners of the stores—have given their permission."

"Great. Thanks. You don't have to hang around," she said when he made no move to go. "I'll shoot down here. Then I can come to your office."

"I've cleared my calendar." He set her bag down, then propped his shoulders against the wall and watched every move she made.

Daisy was used to going about her work single-mindedly forgetting everything and everyone else but the focus of her shots. She was, this time, aware every second of Alex's eyes on her. She tried to tell herself he was just being polite. But he didn't simply watch while she took photos in the stationer's shop and in the electronics store. He followed her outside so she could shoot a couple from down the block.

Daisy shot him a hard look. He smiled back blandly.

"Fine," she muttered, "if you're going to tag along…" Then she raised her voice loud enough for him to hear and motioned him to stand in front of one of the heavy oak and etched glass doors. "Stand there and look 'lord of the manor-ish.'"

He was Greek. What did he know about lords of the manor?

But apparently some things were universal, and he understood perfectly, leaning casually against one of the walls by the front door, a proprietorial air about him that said exactly what she wanted it to—that this was his domain. He owned the place.

"Got it," she said, clicking off half a dozen so she could have her pick.

"Come on upstairs, then." He led the way back inside.

The elevator was utilitarian, so she wasn't sure what to expect when the doors opened—a hallway and doors to offices, she would have guessed. But that wasn't what she got.

The elevator opened into one big room facing north. There were expanses of gleaming oak flooring broken up by areas covered with dove-gray carpet. In one of the carpeted areas, a woman sat at a desk making some notes while she talked on the phone. Not far away, on another carpet there was soft furniture—sofas and armchairs that invited you to sit and peruse books from floor-to-ceiling bookcases.

Where the floor was wood, she saw several large

tables with projects on display, detailed architectural models in place. Around the sides of the room, in their own spaces but accessible to everyone, there were drafting tables, a couple of which had people working at them. They had glanced up when the elevator doors opened, but seeing Alex, they'd nodded and gone back to work.

Daisy's gaze swiveled to take in the whole room. "Wow," she said, impressed. "Very nice."

"I like it. Let me show you around." He introduced her to Alison, his middle-aged office manager. Then he took her to meet the two at the drafting tables. A young dark-haired woman, Naomi, was deeply involved in whatever she'd been assigned and barely glanced up to smile. But the other, an intern named Steve, had some questions about his project, so Daisy was able to take some shots of Alex and Steve, leaning over one of the drafting tables, studying blue prints.

Then, while Alex answered Steve's questions, she wandered around, taking other shots of the room, of Alex on the job.

It was just the way she'd imagined him—in his element, his easy competence apparent. He drew her gaze as he bent over the table, his dark hair falling across his forehead as he pointed out something to Steve. She snapped off a couple of shots. But even when she lowered the camera, she couldn't seem to look away.

"Sorry," he said, coming back to her. "I didn't mean to spend so long with him."

"No problem. I got some good shots. Which is your table?" She nodded toward the vacant drafting tables.

"Upstairs. I'll show you."

He led her to a spiral staircase that ascended in one corner of the room. "We could use the elevator, but this is faster."

It was also a treat. It had caught her eye earlier, a bit of wrought-iron frivolity in stark utilitarian surroundings. And yet it belonged.

"Was it original to the building?" It was a little added lagniappe, and she had already taken a number of shots of it.

"No. But I wanted something to catch the eye," Alex said. "Something that was from the original period. I went to every salvage place in the boroughs, looking. I knew it when I saw it."

"It's perfect." She motioned him to precede her up the steps. "Turn around," she said when he was halfway up. She took several shots of him on the steps, and was seriously tempted to take one of his backside when, afterward, she followed him up.

But she didn't need any more reminders of how tempting Alex Antonides was.

His office was out of the mainstream, but connected to it. "I don't let them up here," he said frankly. "I need my space."

"A perk of being the boss," Daisy acknowledged. But she had to admit she liked his private aerie, too. The room in which he had created his office wasn't large. Like the bigger room downstairs, it had tall, narrow, gothic arched windows and polished oak flooring. Floor-to-ceiling bookshelves held vast arrays of architectural titles, books about design, and a lot of history, art and photography books. Daisy studied the titles.

It was disconcerting to find many of the same titles she had on her own shelves. So, whatever it was, it wasn't just physical.

She wished it were. He would be so much easier to resist. Forcing herself to focus on the task at hand, she gave a little wave of her camera, asking permission to take photos. "May I?"

He nodded. "Of course."

"I've heard that there's a movement to minimize windows for energy conservation," she said as she pointed the camera in his direction. "You obviously don't believe that."

"There's a place for that. But light is good, too.

And while you can conserve energy by building dark, I like light. So I try to make sure the windows are doing their job, too." He stopped. "Sorry. Boring."

Daisy lowered the camera. "It's not, actually. And I'm a photographer. I like light, too."

"Come on," he said suddenly. "I'll show you the best light of all."

Without looking to see if she followed, he started up to the next level on the same spiral staircase. Daisy followed, expecting more office space. But when he reached the landing and unlocked the door, she knew better.

This was where Alex lived.

If he hadn't said, "Welcome to my place," she would have known it anyway. The light walls, the earth tones, the casual modern but not stark furniture, the plush dark rust and blue and gold oriental rug centered on the polished oak floor created a visual backdrop for the man she had known. Even if he weren't standing there watching her take it all in, she would have known this was where he belonged.

There were, in the furnishings, in the books and papers on the coffee table, in the framed architectural drawings on the walls, signs of Alex everywhere. She was shaken by how instantly she felt at home, as if she, too, belonged here.

No. No, she didn't.

She took a breath, steeled herself and tossed his words back at him, "So show me the best light of all."

He smiled. "Right this way."

Wouldn't you just bloody know that it would be the skylight in his bedroom!

Daisy stopped dead at the door, realizing a split second before she crossed the threshold exactly where they were going. "I didn't mean—"

Alex turned, flashing her a grin. "You asked for it."

Daisy read the challenge in it—the very challenge she'd told Cal she could handle. And she could, damn it. So, deliberately, she stepped in and looked around. The skylight was above the bed. The bed looked to be the size of, perhaps, the Sahara Desert—but vastly more comfortable with its buff-colored duvet and a quartet of dark brown pillows.

"Very nice," she said, doing her best to keep her gaze fixed on the skylight until she turned back to the living room again. "Let me shoot some photos out here."

He smiled, but didn't challenge her further, just let her wander around and look her fill.

Daisy resisted looking her fill. She'd have been here for hours, curious about the man, wanting to know him better, at the same time she knew she shouldn't want to know him at all.

Alex's apartment was not some sterile showplace. There were dishes in the sink, a newspaper on the counter. Two pairs of athletic shoes, a gym bag and a racing bike sat by what she supposed was the main front door—the one that didn't lead down to his office. And one wall of the kitchen was painted as a mural of something that looked like the Greek islands—lots of blue sea and sky, white-washed buildings and blue domed churches. It drew her attention.

"Did Martha paint that?"

Martha was Lukas's twin sister. Daisy had met her several times over the years. She knew Martha now lived part of the year in Montana—of all places—and part of the year on Long Island and wherever her husband, Theo Savas, was sailing boats.

It seemed an amazing exotic existence to Daisy who had been born in Colorado, came to the big city for university, and never left—except to go back home occasionally.

"She did," Alex agreed. "Kind of bowls you over, doesn't it?"

"I like it," Daisy said.

"I didn't," Alex said, surprising her.

"What? Why not?"

He shook his head. "Memories."

That startled her until she remembered him telling her about his childhood, about his brother who had died young.

"You could paint over it," she suggested.

He shrugged. "I got used to it. I just wasn't expecting it. I was heading out of town and I told her to paint whatever she wanted. She thought it would make me happy. Can we get on with this?" he said abruptly, gesturing to her camera.

"Oh! Yes, of course!" Daisy grimaced, feeling a flush of confusion engulf her. That would teach her.

She pointed to the armchair near the window. "Go sit there and look at one of your books."

Alex picked up a book and sat down with it, opened it at random, studied it as if he cared what was in it while Daisy moved and shot, moved and shot.

He turned a page. "I hired a matchmaker."

Daisy's finger slipped on the shutter release. Then, taking a slow careful breath so as not to jar the camera, she clicked off several more shots and lowered it again.

"Did you?" she said, heart pounding. "Good for you. I'm sure you'll find exactly what you're looking for. Turn a little more this way."

He turned. "I found her on the internet."

A breath hissed through Daisy's teeth. "The internet? For heaven's sake, Alex! How do you know she's legitimate? She might be a charlatan—someone hanging out her shingle, looking to make money off poor unsuspecting fools."

He looked up from the book and raised a brow. "Poor unsuspecting fools...like me?"

Daisy's cheeks burned. "I didn't mean that! I never said—" She retreated behind her camera again. "I just meant that not everyone is reliable, honest. Did you get letters of recommendation? What do you know about her background?"

"She has a degree in human relations. She was born and raised in Virginia. She came to the 'big city' when she was just out of college. Reminded me a little of you."

"I'm not from Virginia," Daisy bit out. "And I don't have a degree in human relations."

"So maybe she's more qualified than you are," Alex mused, giving her a sly smile.

"Maybe she is. I've got enough here. Let's go

back down to your office." Someplace less intimate. Someplace where she could focus on her work. She didn't want to hear anything more about his matchmaker.

Alex picked up her camera bag, then started down the stairs again. He glanced back. "I went out with one of her suggestions last night."

Daisy pasted on a bright smile. "How nice. Maybe you'll have a wife by Christmas."

He nodded. "Maybe I will. She's a stockbroker. Nice enough. Intense, though," he mused.

Daisy pointed him toward his drafting table. "Put out a drawing and focus," she directed. She did not intend to get sucked into analyzing his date.

"Too intense for me," he went on, even as he obediently pulled out a drawing, spread it on the table and stared down at it. "She'd talked nonstop about everything from chandeliers to parakeets to stock options to astronomy."

"Well, it's early days yet," Daisy said briskly. "Maybe the next one will be better."

If he'd been her client she'd have talked to him about that, tried to learn what he hadn't liked, what was "too intense." But she wasn't finding a wife for Alex Antonides. He was someone else's problem.

He kept his gaze on the drawing. "Maybe. I'm going out with another one tonight."

"Another one?" That fast? Where was the "matchmaking" in that? It sounded more like trial and error.

He glanced around. "Amalie—that's the match-maker—has got a whole list."

A list. Daisy wasn't impressed. "Is she French? Or fake?" she added before she could help herself.

Alex raised a brow. "Her mother's French. Is that a problem?"

Daisy raised her camera again, refusing to admit she was taking refuge behind it. "Of course not. I just wondered. I suppose she's introducing you to French women then." It made sense. He spent a good part of every year in Paris.

"Career women," Alex corrected. "And I'm not looking for a French one. I live here now."

That was news. Daisy stayed behind the camera. She kept moving.

Alex picked up the drawing and rolled it up. Whether she was finished or not, it was clear that he was. "She has a list as long as my arm," he reported. "She said I need options."

Daisy grunted noncommittedly. She didn't think much of "options." But then, when she helped people find the right mate, she was trying to find their soul mate, not a sex partner who was willing to share a mortgage.

"So," Alex said, "I just have to find the right one."

Good luck with that, Daisy thought. But she kept her skepticism to herself. If she expressed it, he'd tell her she should do it herself.

"All done," she said, and began disassembling her camera and stowing it in her bag. "I'll get to work editing these early next week. I'm going to be out all day tomorrow, and I'm not working this weekend. If you'll give me your business card, I'll email you when I've finished. Then you can let me know whether to send you a disk or email you files or send them directly to the magazine."

Alex fished a card out of his wallet, started to hand it to her, then took it back and scribbled something on the back before pressing it into her palm again. "You can reach me at this number anytime."

Not likely. But Daisy just pocketed it and smiled as she zipped her bag shut, stood up and hoisted it onto her shoulder. Then, deliberately, she stuck out her hand to Alex for a businesslike shake. "Thank you."

He blinked, then stared—at her, at her hand. Something unreadable flickered across his face.

Then in slow motion, he reached out and took her fingers in his. Flesh on flesh.

Daisy tried not to think about it. But his palm was warm and firm and there were light calluses on it, as if he didn't only sit in his office and draw. She remembered those calluses, those fingers—the way they had grazed her skin, had traced the line of her jaw, the curve of her hip, the hollow of her collarbone. Other lines. Other hollows.

She swallowed hard.

Still he held her hand. Then abruptly he dropped it. "Thank you, too," he said, his voice crisp. As businesslike as she hoped hers was.

"Goodbye." One more polite smile and she'd be gone.

Alex nodded, his gaze fixed on hers. The phone on his desk rang. He grimaced, then picked it up. "What is it, Alison?" There was barely concealed impatience in his tone. Then he grimaced again. "Right. Okay. Give me a sec." He turned back to Daisy. "I have to take this."

"Of course. I was just on my way."

She was down the steps and out the door without looking back. There. She'd done it—beard the lion in his den.

And survived.

Just like she'd told Cal she would.

* * *

Staring at the skylight in his ceiling in the dark didn't have much to recommend it. There were stars. There were a few small clouds scudding along, silvery in the moonlight.

There was Daisy.

Alex flipped over and dragged the pillow over his head. It didn't help. She was on the insides of his eyelids, it seemed.

The whole day had been a bloody disaster. Well, no, that wasn't true. Before 3:00 p.m., things had been pretty normal. He'd been a little distracted, there had been a lot to do, but he'd got some work done.

And then Daisy had shown up. Exactly as he'd planned.

She was supposed to come, take her photos, and leave again. He was supposed to smile and look professional and competent and disinterested, and see her on her way. Asking her to take the photos was supposed to settle things between them, put them on a business footing.

It was supposed to pigeonhole her—and convince Alex that he wasn't really attracted, that he hadn't been thinking about her fifty times a day since he'd seen her again, that she didn't draw his gaze more than any other woman, that he was perfectly happy to watch her walk out of his office and out of his life.

The operative word was *supposed*. The truth was, well, something else altogether.

And the day hadn't been all that normal before three o'clock, either. He might have got some work done earlier in the day, but shortly before Daisy was due to arrive, he'd found himself walking over to look out the window every few minutes. It was a nice day, sunny, brisk. He was enjoying perfect fall weather. No more, no less.

So why had his heart kicked over at the sight of her down there on the sidewalk, pointing her camera up at his building? Why had he stopped Steve abruptly halfway through a question to go down and intercept her before she came in? Why had his fingers itched to reach out and touch her? And why had he had to fight to suppress the urge to kiss her when she'd turned and bumped straight into his chest?

She drove him crazy. She got under his skin. The minute he saw her, he couldn't seem to focus on anything or anyone else.

The feeling persisted the whole time she was there—this desire to touch her, to smooth a hand over her hair, to pull her against him, to touch his lips to hers. His heart had begun hammering the moment he'd seen her, and it was still banging away when he'd had to take that phone call and she'd left.

He'd wanted to stop her, to say, "Hang on. Wait," because it was too soon, there had been so little time, he had not had enough of her yet.

But at the same time, he knew it was stupid—*he* was stupid.

Daisy Harris—Connolly!—was *not* what he wanted—or needed—in his life.

And it didn't matter that she was divorced now. She still apparently wanted things he didn't want. Wanted things he wasn't prepared to give. So the one bit of common sense he had, had kept his mouth shut.

He hadn't said, "Wait." Hadn't stopped her or called her to come back.

It was better she had left. And better still that he had had a date that night with one of Amalie's "options."

Whoever she was, she would erase Daisy from his mind.

Except she hadn't.

Her name was Laura or Maura or Dora. Hell, he couldn't remember. She had been pleasant enough in an airheaded sort of way. But he'd spent the evening making mental comparisons between her and Daisy.

Suffice to say, Dora/Maura/Laura had come up short on all counts.

She didn't have Daisy's charm. She didn't have Daisy's ability to listen. She didn't have Daisy's smile or Daisy's sparkling eyes or Daisy's eager enthusiasm.

She wasn't Daisy. He was bored.

He'd been polite enough. He'd listened and nodded and smiled until his jaw ached. He'd dutifully told her a bit about himself, but his comments were flat and uninteresting even to his own ears. It wasn't hard to tell she was bored, too.

"You win a few, you lose a few," she'd said, smiling and shaking his hand when they'd left the restaurant to go their separate ways.

It was nine-thirty. Shortly after ten he was home.

And that was when he began to realize his mistake. He'd not only lost, he'd lost big-time.

He hadn't vanquished Daisy from his mind by having her come take photos this afternoon. On the contrary he now had a whole host of new images of Daisy—on his turf.

Now when he stood at the window, he could look down at where he'd first spotted her, camera to her eye, taking pictures of his building, her hair loose in the wind. And when he grew tired of pacing his apartment and went back down to his office to do some work, the minute he sat down at his drafting table, he could almost feel her presence just over his right shoulder where she had been that afternoon.

He crumpled up half a dozen attempted drawings before he gave up, stomped back upstairs, stripped off his clothes and took a shower.

She hadn't been in his shower, at least.

Not this one, anyway. But he'd shared a shower with her five years ago, and the memories flashed across his mind with such insistence that he'd cranked the hot water down till only the cold beat down on his body. But his arousal persisted.

He wanted to go for a bike ride, burn off the energy, the edge. But not in Brooklyn. Not at midnight. There was stupid—and then there was stupid.

He was stupid, not suicidal.

He should have known better than to think he could see her again and forget her. He'd never been able to forget her. And he wouldn't be able to, damn it, until Amalie finally found him the right woman.

In the meantime he'd flung himself onto his bed,

stared up at the skylight—and discovered the depth of his folly.

Daisy had been in his bedroom. He'd deliberately brought her in here—to show her the "best light"—wanting to get a rise out of her.

Well, she wasn't the one who was rising. Pun intended, he thought savagely. The joke was on him.

The trouble with doing an hour-long shoot with Alex was that the hour was just the beginning.

Oh, it was over for him. But Daisy had to work with the images, study them, analyze them, choose the best ones, correct them. Spend hours and hours and hours contemplating them.

It drove her insane.

She didn't want to see him in his element hour after hour. She didn't want to feast her eyes on that handsome face. She didn't want to focus on the lithe muscular body as he stretched across the drafting table to point something out to Steve. She didn't want to study the strong profile, the sharp angles, the hard jaw, and hawklike nose as he stared out the window.

He was everything she'd thought he would become.

And she couldn't bear to look at it.

She put the photos away and went to read books

to Charlie. The next night she watched a movie instead. The following night she had a new shoot, some high school senior pictures to work on. She'd get to Alex's when the memory of being in his office, in his apartment—in his bedroom—wasn't quite so immediate.

She would do them.

Not now. Not yet.

She needed time. An eon or two.

She needed space. Would a galaxy be enough?

The trouble with the "options" Amalie was providing him with, Alex decided after his fifth disastrous date, was that not one of them—so far—had been worth the trouble.

He'd gone out with half a dozen since he'd contracted with her, and since the intense Gina whom he'd mentioned to Daisy and the airhead whose name he couldn't recall, there had been phlegmatic Deirdre and twitchy Shannon and a politician called Chloe.

But if they'd been bad, tonight's "flavor of the evening" was absolutely no improvement, though Amalie had sworn they would be perfect for each other.

"She's an architecture student. You'll have so much in common!" Amalie had vowed.

He met her at a restaurant near the Lincoln Center. She was at the bar when he got there, a red scarf looped around her neck. That's how he would recognize her, she'd told him on the phone.

He did a double take when he saw her. She looked so much like Daisy. Maybe a little blonder than Daisy, maybe a little taller. And her eyes were a sort of faded gray-green. She beamed at him when he arrived.

"I knew it was you!" She was like bubbly champagne. "You're even more handsome than your picture."

She might have meant it. He didn't know. Didn't care. Her eyes didn't sparkle like Daisy's.

They took their drinks to a table and he said, "Amalie says you're studying architecture."

Not quite. What Tracie knew about architecture she appeared to have memorized from Wikipedia. She started talking about the Acropolis before they ordered and had barely reached the Colosseum by the time their entrees arrived.

It was always interesting to learn which buildings inspired another architect, but Tracie wasn't an architect—or even a student of architecture, Alex was willing to bet. After two hours of her nonstop talking, he'd had enough. If she hadn't looked so much like Daisy, he doubted he'd have lasted that long.

But the truth was, the longer he spent with her, the less like Daisy she seemed. Tracie was nervous, edgy. She had a shrill laugh. Her voice grated on him.

Daisy's laugh made him feel like smiling. Her eyes always sparkled—either with joy or annoyance. It didn't matter which. They drew his gaze. When she was with him, he couldn't stop looking at her. Her voice was always like warm honey.

Not, of course, that he'd heard it since she'd walked out of his place a week and a half ago. She'd taken his picture and said she'd be in touch and he'd never heard from her again.

He set down his fork sharply.

"You're bored," Tracie accused, staring hard at him over his empty plate. He hadn't had to talk, so he'd eaten everything in front of him.

Now Alex shook his head. "No," he lied. "I'm distracted. I just realized I have to be somewhere. I have an appointment."

"Tonight?" Her eyes widened.

"I have to pick up some photos," he said. "I need to get them to an editor in the morning." It wasn't entirely true. But the editor did need them. She'd called him yesterday inquiring about where they were. He'd thought Daisy had sent them in so she wouldn't have to contact him again.

Tracie pursed her lips, then pouted. "But we've only reached the Duomo." Which meant they had about six hundred more years of architecture to cover.

"I'm sorry," Alex said firmly. "I really need to go."

He did finish his coffee, but then called for the bill, saw her into a taxi and watched it drive off. Not until it disappeared around the corner did he breathe a sigh of relief. He was free.

For what?

It was just past nine. Not really late—unless you'd just spent the past two hours being systematically bored to death. Then you wanted some excitement, something to get the adrenaline going.

But the adrenaline was already going—and so were his feet.

They knew exactly where they were headed, and before Alex even realized it, he was on the corner of the street where Daisy's office was.

Daisy—who was, let's face it, the reason he'd been willing to go on five dates in the past ten days—so he would bloody well stop thinking about her.

But he hadn't stopped.

Every night he lay in bed and stared at the damned skylight and remembered her sparkling eyes, her smooth golden skin, her warm smile. And because he was in bed, he remembered other things, too.

He remembered touching her skin—all over. He remembered kissing her smiling mouth. He remembered stripping off her clothes and running his hands over her body, teasing, tasting—

Hell! He couldn't show up on her doorstep halfway to wanting to bed her. Not that she'd even be there. It was her office, for God's sake. Why would she be burning the midnight oil editing photos? Presumably she had a life.

She probably even went out on dates now that she was divorced. Maybe she had a boyfriend. His jaw tightened and he shoved his hands in the pockets of his jacket as he started walking down the street.

He didn't expect she would be there. So he was taken aback to discover lights on in the bay window of the apartment that was her office.

She didn't have a life, after all? He stopped across the street and stared.

Now what? Turn around and walk back to Columbus? Catch a cab home? And stare at the damn skylight again?

Abruptly Alex crossed the street, took the steps to the front door two at a time, opened the door to the vestibule and punched the doorbell.

He waited. And waited. He shifted from one foot to the other, and wondered if she left the lights on all the time. Maybe she wasn't even there.

He was ready to turn around and leave when all at once he heard the sound of the lock twisting and the door handle rattling. The door opened.

Daisy stared out at him, nonplused. *"Alex?"*

"I came for the photos."

"What?"

"The editor called me. She wants the photos. You said you'd have them ready."

"I said I'd call you when they were ready." She was gripping the door, glaring at him, and by God, yes, her eyes were sparking fire.

He almost smiled as he snaked past her into her office before she could object, then turned and let his gaze run over her again.

She was wearing a pair of jeans and a sweat-shirt—about as inelegant as imaginable—and she looked as sexy as hell. Her blonde hair was hanging loose around her face. It was disheveled, as if she—or someone else?—had been running fingers through it.

"Am I interrupting something?" he snapped.

"What?" She frowned. Then she shrugged. "My work. If you want the photos, let me get back to them. They're not done yet. I'm sorry. I've been busy. I'll have them for you tomorrow. I—"

"Let me see them."

"No. Not while I'm still working."

"Why? Afraid of someone else's opinion?"

"Do I offer you opinions about the buildings you design?" she countered with saccharine sweetness. "Of course not. So go away."

But Alex didn't want to go away. He wanted to drop down in the chair and watch her work. He wanted to run his fingers through her hair and pull her close. He wanted to slide his hands down the curve of her spine, cup her buttocks—

He groaned.

"What's wrong?" She was looking at him intently, worriedly.

He ground his teeth, then turned away, knowing he should get the hell out of here, but somehow he couldn't go. It was as if she'd bewitched him, cast some spell that wouldn't let him find the woman he knew had to be out there, the woman who would actually be right for him.

"Alex?" she pressed in the face of his silence.

Finally he snapped. "I've had five dates, and they've all been disasters!"

Daisy's eyes widened. She stared at him, then let out a sound that might have been a laugh. Or a snort.

"What a shame," Daisy said in a tone that told him it had been both a laugh and a snort.

"It is, damn it! And it's a waste of time." Alex cracked his knuckles and spun away to pace irritably around her office. But every step brought him closer to her. And he wanted her. Badly.

She stepped past him and moved toward her desk, and he wheeled to follow her when he found himself face-to-face with the photos on her walls.

None of them, of course, was Daisy.

But they all spoke of Daisy. Of what she wanted and he didn't.

Families. Children. Pets.

He looked at her. Her cheeks were flushed. She ran her tongue over her lips. She watched him warily, worriedly.

"Never mind," he said abruptly. "I have to go."

Ignoring his desire, forcing himself to turn away from the most beautiful woman he'd ever made love to, he stalked out the door. He was halfway down the steps when he turned his head, his heart still hammering. "Send me those photos, damn it."

CHAPTER FIVE

THE next day Alex got an email with a link to a site where he could download the photos Daisy had taken.

Here you are, the email said. Sorry it took so long. Hope they meet with your editor's satisfaction. Thank you for the opportunity to work with you.

Kind regards, Daisy Connolly.

Kind regards? Daisy *Connolly*?

As if he would need her last name to distinguish her from all the other Daisys in his life.

Blast her, anyway! Alex smacked a hand on the desk next to his computer screen. So all it had needed was for him to turn up on her doorstep and make an idiot of himself and Daisy was suddenly inspired to finish editing the photos, send them along and get him out of her life.

Swell.

He'd lain awake half the night—staring at the damned skylight and cursing his own misplaced desire—and wishing Amalie would come up with a viable "option."

In the morning he called her and demanded a better selection. "The last one was a charlatan," he said. "If she was an architecture student, I play center field for the New York Yankees."

"I'm talking to another young woman today," she promised. "You're very discerning. It takes time."

It didn't take time, damn it. That was the trouble. If Daisy wanted what he wanted there wouldn't be any problem at all.

But she didn't. That was perfectly clear. She probably hadn't been stalling. She'd probably actually been busy, too busy to get right to his photos. But once he'd turned up on her doorstep, making demands, she'd outdone herself getting the photos finished so she didn't need to have anything more to do with him.

They were amazing photos, though.

He stood in his office, staring at them now. He'd spread them out on his drafting table, studying them, seeing himself through her eyes.

They were every bit as sharp and insightful as the ones he'd seen on her wall last night. She'd taken most of the shots in black and white which, on first glance, surprised him.

But the more he studied them, the more he saw

what she was doing: she had used the monochrome scheme to pare him down to his essence, exactly the way an architectural drawing or a blueprint did.

She caught him clearly—a man who had little patience with subtlety, who knew what he wanted.

He wanted her.

She had to know that. Didn't she know that?

He sighed and scraped the photos into a pile and put them back into the envelope. Of course she knew it.

She didn't want him—not on his terms.

So he'd seen the last of her.

End of story.

Daisy was still taking deep breaths and letting them out slowly a week later. But it was her own fault. She knew she should have got the photos edited and sent off right away. She hadn't.

And so Alex had turned up on her doorstep. An intense, edgy, irritated Alex. An Alex who had looked at her with fire in his normally cool green gaze. An Alex who had shot into her office so quickly, she hadn't even thought about how to stop him. And once he was there, it had felt like being trapped in a cage with a full-grown, very hungry panther.

A panther who had complained about the meals he was being offered at the same time he was looking at her like he intended to make her the next one.

She'd skittered away, crossed the room, needing to put space between them, because the mere sight of him had set her heart to pounding. All her senses went on alert with Alex. Her body wanted him no matter what her brain—and her mother's-heart—told her was wise.

She had been determined to resist—not just Alex, but her own desire.

Then abruptly he had turned and walked out!

And Daisy had been left staring after him as he strode off into the cold dark windy night. Then she'd shut the door and leaned against it, her heart still slamming against the wall of her chest, her pulse racing.

The adrenaline had kept her working half the night.

It took a week to wear off, more for her to be able to say with confidence to Cal that life was back to normal, and still more until she believed it herself.

So it was a blow on the first Saturday evening in November to hear a knock on the door, expect to get the Thai takeaway she'd ordered, and find Alex standing on her doorstep again.

She stared at him, dumbstruck.

"Good evening to you, too," he said cheerfully. His tone was mild, friendly, completely at odds with the Alex who had shown up last time.

"Good evening," she replied cautiously, trying not to look at his smooth-shaven face, his quirking smile, that groove in his cheek she always itched to touch. Deliberately she curled her fingers into the palm of her hand.

He hesitated a split second, then said, "I just wanted to say that I may have found the one."

Daisy blinked. "The one? The one what?"

His smile widened. "Woman." There was a pause. Then, "Wife," he clarified.

Daisy's stomach did an odd sort of somersault. She swallowed, then mustered her best polite smile. "Really. How nice."

She shut her eyes for an instant, and opened them to discover that he'd done it again—slipped past her and was suddenly standing in her office. How did he do that?

"She's a vice president in marketing for an international cosmetics firm," he reported, his handsome face looking very pleased. "She runs campaigns in half a dozen places all over the world. Always on the move. She has two phones.

A red one for emergencies." He grinned, as if this were a good thing.

"Does she?" Daisy said drily. "Sounds perfect for you."

"You think so, too?" He was still grinning, so she didn't know if he heard her sarcasm as it had been intended or not. "That's what I thought. I read Amalie the riot act after the first bunch, said if that was as good as she could do, I was finished. And then she came up with Caroline."

Caroline. Even her name was right. Sophisticated, but approachable. She did sound perfect.

"And," Alex went on with considerable enthusiasm, "there are other things, too—she's beautiful, bright, funny, articulate, well-read."

Daisy shut the door but stayed by it, keeping an eye out for the Thai deliveryman and thanking God that Charlie was at Cal's this weekend. "So have you asked her to marry you yet?" she asked Alex flippantly.

"Considering it."

Her jaw dropped. "On the basis of a couple of dates?"

"Three," Alex corrected. He was moving around her office in panther mode, but looking better fed. He picked up an alabaster cat on the bookcase, and examined it while he talked. "Well, two and a half." His mouth twisted wryly. "The red phone rang tonight. She had to leave in the middle of dinner. She's on her way to San Francisco right now."

"You're joking." He had to be joking. *Didn't he?*

But when he didn't immediately agree that he was, Daisy shook her head, torn between despair and the prickling of awareness and wholly useless desire she always felt faced with Alexandros Antonides. Still. Damn it. "You're insane."

He put the cat down again and looked at her quizzically. "Insane? Why?"

"You can't make a decision like that in a few weeks' time!"

"Why not? She's what I want."

"But are *you* what *she* wants?" Daisy didn't know why she was asking that. Didn't know why she was arguing with him.

"That's her problem."

"Yours, too." She couldn't seem to help herself. "If you get married without knowing each other well, without thinking things through—"

"I could end up like you did?"

Daisy rocked with the punch of his words. *"What?"*

"That isn't why your marriage didn't work?"

"No, of course it isn't!" Daisy felt the heat of his accusation. But she denied it, and it wasn't a lie, either. "And we're not discussing my marriage." She wrapped her arms across her chest, as if they would defend her. Fat chance.

"Why didn't it, then?" he persisted.

"This is not about me!"

He raised his brows. "Maybe I'm trying to learn from your mistake."

"You and I are not likely to make the same mistakes."

Alex shrugged. "How will I know if you don't tell me?"

"I'm not going to tell you, Alex! My marriage is none of your business." She shoved away from the door and jerked it open. "I think you should go."

But Alex didn't go anywhere. On the contrary, he turned and flopped down into one of the armchairs, settling in, folding his arms behind his head. "Not yet. I want to hear why I shouldn't pop the question."

Daisy wanted to strangle him. But the quickest way to get him out of her life was to answer his questions. So she did. "Because," she said slowly and with the articulation of an elocution teacher, "you don't want to get a divorce. Do you?" she challenged him. "Maybe you don't care whether you do or not because you won't care about her."

"I don't want a divorce," he said evenly. The green eyes glinted.

Daisy shrugged. "Fine. Then take your time. Make sure you're on the same page. That you want the same things. That... Oh, hell, why am I telling you this? You don't understand!"

He cocked his head. "Weren't you on the same page, Daisy?" He sounded almost sympathetic now.

She pressed her lips together and didn't answer.

He gave her a little half smile. "Are you going to marry again?"

"I doubt it." She turned away, then turned back and shrugged. "Maybe someday. It depends."

"On?"

"On whether or not I'm in love with him."

Alex's jaw clenched.

Daisy smiled. It was a painful smile, hard-earned. "Yes, love. Still. I want the whole package, Alex. Now more than ever."

Alex didn't move. A muscle ticking in his temple was the only betrayal of anything beyond casual interest in what she had to say. Then, with studied nonchalance, he rose slowly. "I wish you the joy of it then."

"And I you," Daisy said automatically.

He gave her a sardonic look.

"No, truly." She almost put a hand on his arm as he passed. But then she laced her fingers together instead. Still, she looked up at him earnestly. "I mean it, Alex. You deserve a wonderful life. I hope…Caroline is the right woman for you. I hope she gives you what you want."

He had stopped and was standing now, quite close. She kept her gaze on the rise and fall of his chest, knew that she could reach out and touch him. Knew she should back away.

But she didn't. She stayed quite still and met his gaze. "Regardless of what you think, marriage is more than you expect. You should…take your time, get to know this…woman you're considering marrying. Make sure it's right for both of you."

Alex stood staring at her as if he couldn't believe the words coming out of her mouth.

Daisy couldn't believe them, either. It wasn't any of her business. But she couldn't seem to stop herself. And maybe she did owe him the benefit of her experience with Cal. Certainly it had taught her something.

"No matter what you think you want out of marriage," she finished, "it can surprise you. You shouldn't take it lightly."

Alex's eyes narrowed further, and she expected he would tell her to mind her own business. But his jaw just tightened again, then he nodded. "I'll keep it in mind."

Their gazes locked—all the electricity flowing through New York City at that moment had nothing on what arced between them.

Then, carefully, consciously, Daisy swallowed. "Have a good life, Alex."

For a long moment he didn't reply, and she couldn't read his gaze. Then he said flatly, "I will. Shall I invite you to the wedding?"

No! It was her gut-level response. But she squelched it. "When you're sure she's the right one," she said slowly, "I would be delighted to come."

Alex's lips pressed together in a thin line. He nodded, then walked past her wordlessly out the door.

She closed it after him, leaned back against it, knees wobbling. Only after the sound of his footsteps had long faded away, did Daisy breathe again.

Moving on.

That's what her father always used to say when Daisy or her sister got all wrought up about something they could do nothing about. He'd listen to them anguishing for, oh, maybe thirty minutes, and then he'd say, "Can you do anything about it?"

They'd say, "No."

And he'd flash them his sunny grin and say, "So...moving on..."

He didn't mean, *get over it*. He meant, *stop dwelling on it. Get past it.*

You might still ache with disappointment. You might remember it forever. But you'd done all you could do. Now it was time to pull up your socks and move on.

Daisy moved on.

She still thought about Alex. How could she not? She had loved him once. He was the father of her child, even if he didn't know it. She owed him for that—for Charlie. And she wished things could have been different.

But they weren't.

Life moved on, and determinedly Daisy moved on with it. She did her work. She introduced a great couple, Debbie whom she'd met at a yoga class and Mark, who played baseball with Cal, and was delighted when they seemed to hit it off. She wasn't losing her touch with other people at least. Cal bought Charlie a point-and-shoot camera, and she went with the two of them for walks in the park and on the streets and took loads of pictures. It was fun to discover Charlie's interest, and restful to be with him and Cal.

Every time her thoughts drifted to Alex and she wondered if he'd proposed yet, she deliberately focused them elsewhere. So she wasn't even thinking about him the Sunday evening before Thanksgiving when Cal came into the kitchen and asked, "Whatever happened with Alex?"

Her ex had stopped by that afternoon to take Charlie for a bike ride in the park. When they'd come back, Daisy had invited him to stay for leftovers. After, he'd helped Charlie build a fire station with his Legos. Now Charlie had gone upstairs to get ready for his bath while Daisy put dishes in the dishwasher.

She felt a moment's jolt at the sound of his name. But then she just shrugged. "No idea. Haven't seen him for a while. I believe he's got a woman in his life. He seems to think she's 'the one.'" Daisy couldn't help adding that.

Cal looked at her closely. "I'm sorry."

"I'm not," Daisy said, dropping forks in the silverware slots. "He was never the man I thought he was. He still isn't."

"Life sucks," Cal said with a faint grin.

"It has some good bits," Daisy countered, nodding toward the stairs where they could both hear Charlie banging around in the upstairs hall.

Cal's grin widened. "You're right. It does." He

shoved away from the doorjamb and flexed his shoulders. "I'll be going then. Thanks for letting me take him to the park."

"Anytime." She walked to the front door with him and kissed him on the cheek and he gave her a hug. Then he shrugged on his jacket. "I'll pick Charlie up Thursday morning. I told my folks we'd be up there by noon."

Daisy nodded and forced a smile even as she felt her throat tighten. "He'll have so much fun."

Cal was taking Charlie to his parents' upstate for Thanksgiving. They wouldn't be back until Sunday morning. The thought of rattling around by herself for four days was horrible. But it was good for Charlie and for Cal and his family. It was a part of the life they'd made.

"My folks are really looking forward to it," Cal said. He looked at her closely. "You can come if you want." He must have seen some of the hollowness she felt.

Daisy shook her head. "Thanks, but I can't. You know that."

If she did Cal's parents might think there was hope of them getting back together. They had been upset when she and Cal divorced. Now they seemed to be coming to terms with the way things were. It wouldn't do to get their hopes up again.

"You're probably right. No, you are right. It's just—I'm sorry. Especially this year."

Daisy shrugged. "Don't worry. I'll be fine. I'm going to Finn and Izzy's. It will be chaos. I'll never miss you. What do you have planned?"

"Going fishing if the weather stays warm enough. Chopping wood otherwise. Getting ready for winter." He grimaced.

"You'll have fun."

"Charlie will make it fun. He and Dad are something else when you get them together." Cal shook his head, grinning. "Like two kids."

"I'd guess there were three." Daisy cocked her head and smiled at him.

Cal rubbed a hand against the back of his neck. "Well, yeah."

Their eyes met, both of them rueful.

"Moving on," Daisy said with all the briskness she could muster.

And Cal nodded resolutely. "Moving on."

He went out, and Daisy locked the door after him. Then she went back into the living room, rubbing her hands up and down her arms. Was Alex having Thanksgiving with the woman in his life? Or was he working on one continent while she was on another?

What did she care? Daisy asked herself irritably.

She didn't, damn it. But sometimes moving on felt curiously like walking through molasses with her shoelaces tied together. Hard and lonely.

She felt suddenly very, very cold.

CHAPTER SIX

FINN and Izzy's at Thanksgiving *was* chaos. Finn's nieces, Tansy and Pansy, were both there, along with Rip and Crash, Finn and Izzy's sons, and a dozen or so other friends, several slightly giddy from having spent the night before over by the Museum of Natural History where all the gigantic balloon floats for the annual parade were being inflated.

Daisy had gone to the MacCauleys' early and she'd stayed late. Friday she'd spent the entire day catching up on photo editing. More often than she'd liked, she'd been tempted to open the folder where Alex's photos were.

Every time, she'd steeled herself against it and had resisted.

Saturday was harder. Her backlog of work was gone. The house was reasonably clean. The laundry was done, folded, put away. The rugs vacuumed, the furniture dusted. She supposed she could clean the oven, but that seemed like taking things too far.

Instead she took the dog Murphy for a long walk in the park, then decided to do some Christmas shopping. Closer to Christmas, stores would be jammed. Of course, they were on Saturday, too. But it wasn't as lonely as being home by herself, wondering if Charlie and Cal were having a good time.

Wondering what Alex was doing.

It was a relief when Cal and Charlie got back late Sunday afternoon. Charlie was full of stories about hiking in the woods and stacking firewood.

"No, I didn't let him chop it," Cal said before she could ask.

"An' we caught fish," Charlie told her, hopping from one foot to the other. "We got pictures. Look."

Daisy admired the pictures Cal had taken of Charlie and the fish. One of them, though, startled her as his expression in it was so much like Alex's. She never thought he looked like Alex. She really didn't know who he looked like, except that he had her color hair. But in that photo of him grinning up at his grandfather she could see that he had Alex's profile. It made her catch her breath.

"What's wrong?" Cal asked.

"Nothing," she said, papering over her surprise. "I was just amazed at the size of the fish."

"It was huuuuuge," Charlie told her proudly. He spread his arms to their fullest extent.

"Well, maybe not quite that big," Cal said.

But to Charlie it was the biggest fish in the world, and he'd had the best time in the world. And he proceeded to tell Daisy all about it after Cal went home and all through dinner and during his bath.

And Daisy nodded and smiled as she listened to her son's nonstop commentary. He'd had a wonderful time. She was glad he had gone. Glad Cal and his parents had had the joy of him.

Mostly, though, she was glad he was home again.

And when she went to bed that night, she thought, *I can do this. I'm going to be fine.*

She and Cal could cope with trading Charlie back and forth. Charlie wasn't a basket case. He was a normal happy little boy. Life was good.

She didn't think about Alex—or his perfect woman.

At least she tried not to.

"How much longer till Christmas?" Charlie asked. He'd been asking for the past four days, ever since he'd got back from Cal's parents'.

"Oh, a long time," Daisy said, tucking him into

bed. She'd been saying the same thing every day since, too, because a person who was Almost Five had no concept of time, and she'd quickly discovered that if she said "soon," Charlie expected it to be "right after lunch."

"And my birthday?"

"Not quite as long."

Charlie made a face. "They should hurry up."

"All in good time." Even though she had caught up on things over Thanksgiving already, four days later, she felt her to-do lists getting longer by the minute. Lots of people suddenly remembered they wanted family photos for Christmas, and Daisy, understanding the desire, tried not to disappoint any of them.

She had other jobs, too. Most were from repeat customers who wanted her to do some editorial work, and a promo for a boutique in Soho. But one phone call the day after Thanksgiving had surprised her.

"This is Lauren Nicols," the woman had said when Daisy answered. "You did the photos for my piece on Alexandros Antonides."

"Oh! Yes, of course. I hope they were suitable," Daisy said, her heart quickening.

"More than," Lauren Nicols said warmly. "I was delighted. Alex told me you'd be good, but they were better than I'd hoped. The black and white surprised me, but it was perfect. You caught the man."

"I hope so," Daisy said honestly. "I tried."

"Oh, you did," the other woman assured her. "I wondered if you'd be willing to do some more for me."

"Of Alex?" Daisy asked, startled.

"No, Alex's article is in production. But I do other personality pieces for trade periodicals, usually three or four a month. Would you be interested in working with me on a couple of them at least?"

"I—" Daisy stopped herself before she could refuse, because really, why should she? She had enjoyed doing the photo shoot of Alex, and what better way to make sure her brain kept him in the "business" folder of her mind than to start filling it with other assignments, as well? "Yes," she had said. "I'd like that."

And so she had two shoots for Lauren to do before the holidays, as well.

"Go to sleep," she told Charlie now. "It will get here sooner."

"How much sooner?"

Daisy bent and kissed him good night. "You'll just have to wait and see."

Charlie made a face. But eventually he screwed

his eyes shut, and Daisy, knowing that was going to be his best attempt, smiled and turned out the light. "Night, Chaz," she said softly. Then she pulled the door and went down the hall to her office where she'd be working until midnight at least.

First on the docket were the wedding photos she'd taken last night. Wednesday night weddings weren't common, but this had been a small intimate affair to which Daisy had been thrilled to be invited—and eager to take the photos.

They were her wedding present to the couple because both the bride and the groom were "hers."

Seeing Rafaela Cruz, a tech at Murphy's veterinarian's office, and Gino Martinelli, a cop who lived in Finn MacCauley's building, standing at the altar together made Daisy's heart sing for she had helped them find each other.

When she'd learned that besides being a photographer, Daisy was a matchmaker, Rafaela had said, "Huh. Not sure I believe in that."

"Some people don't," Daisy had replied. She wasn't in the market to twist anyone's arm. But Rafaela had wanted to know more because, as she said, "I don't believe there's any good men left." So Daisy had spent time talking to her, trying to discover who, beneath her bluster, Rafaela really was.

Even when she finally said she wanted to try it, Rafaela had had her doubts.

And she and Gino had definitely not been "love at first sight."

Gino, who was Rip MacCauley's soccer coach, had been badly burned in an earlier relationship. But somehow he was the one Daisy had thought of when Rafaela had challenged her to "prove there's one good man."

"Come watch him coach," Daisy had suggested.

Rafaela had dismissed the idea. "I don't want a coach. I want a husband."

"You want a patient man," Daisy said. "A man who works hard and values kids and will be there for you and your family no matter what."

"Yes, but—" Rafaela had protested.

"Maybe Gino could be that man. Unless you're afraid to try?" Daisy had challenged her right back. Then she'd turned around and challenged a reluctant Gino, too.

"She's too pretty," Gino had said. "She'll want some hotshot stud."

Daisy had just looked him up and down. "And you're not a stud?"

Gino had laughed at that. "All right. Bring her on."

They'd been cautious to the point that Daisy

sometimes wanted to bang their heads together. But gradually Rafaela and Gino had faced their doubts, had given each other a shot. Had discovered in each other what Daisy had seen from early days. Over the summer they had fallen in love.

And now they were married.

Daisy's gift to them was going to be a book of photos she'd taken throughout their courtship and at their wedding. She just needed to get it finished. The pages from the courtship were done. Now she picked up the wedding invitation and set it on the flatbed scanner. It was high rag content paper, heavy and elegant.

Daisy remembered when she'd plucked it out of the mailbox right before Thanksgiving. She had stared at it, feeling an odd sinking sensation in the pit of her stomach because she hadn't thought it was Rafaela and Gino's invitation at all.

She'd thought it was Alex's.

She'd been shocked at the relief she'd felt upon opening it to discover Rafaela's and Gino's names inside.

Of course, she'd told herself logically, even if Alex had run right out and asked his perfect woman to marry him the minute he'd left her that night, they wouldn't have been sending out invitations right away.

But logic had never had much to do with anything where her relationship with Alex was concerned.

Now, taking an expansive breath, Daisy smoothed the invitation flat and lowered the lid, then pushed the scanning button.

The phone rang as it was appearing on her screen. She picked it up absently. "Daisy Connolly."

"Daisy." The voice was gruff and instantly recognizable. "I have a favor to ask."

"Alex," she said as soon as she could breathe again. "What do you want?"

"A date."

Once more Daisy's breath caught in her throat. Then she realized what he was really asking for. "I am not matchmaking for you."

"I don't want you to fix me up with a date. I want you."

I want you. She knew he didn't mean it the way it sounded. She didn't *want* him to mean it the way it sounded. But she didn't know what he did mean, either. *"What are you talking about?"*

"I need a date for Saturday night."

"Need a date?" That had to be a first.

"There's a big charity fundraising dinner and dance at the Plaza. Remember I told you I designed a new wing for a hospital? Well, I'm on the guest list—and they're giving me some plaque or something—so I have to show up. With a date."

Daisy waited a beat. "What happened to Caroline?"

"Caroline had to fly out to Hong Kong this afternoon. Unexpected breakdown of some project she'd been overseeing. She won't be back for a week. I can't show up alone. I've already committed for two. They expect me to bring someone. Head table and all that."

"Head table?"

He grunted. "So I need a replacement." And apparently in his mind it was perfectly logical that she would drop everything and accompany him to some society event in another woman's place.

Daisy focused on the wedding invitation on her screen. "Get your matchmaker to find you one."

"Can't."

"Of course you can."

"No," Alex said tersely. "I can't. Thanks to you."

That startled her. "Me? Why me?"

"Because, damn it, you're the one who told me to take it slow. 'Don't ask her to marry you yet. Get to know her,' you said. Make sure she's 'the one.'"

He'd listened?

"So I have been. It isn't easy because half the

time I'm out of town or she is. But we've gone out more."

"As well you should," Daisy said firmly, still surprised that he'd done it.

"So I can't ask Amalie to find me a date, can I?" Alex said. "If I went out with someone else now—someone new—what would that say to Caroline? Not to mention that I'd be creating false expectations in whoever Amalie found."

Daisy was somewhere between dazed and amazed. "You thought of that all by yourself?" Since when had Alex put thought into the repercussions of relationships?

"Can I help it if you put ideas in my head?"

"Good for me." She grinned in spite of herself.

"So you see the problem. It has to be you."

Daisy pressed back against the desk chair she sat in and asked, "Why won't I upset Caroline?"

"She knows I need a date. I told her I was going to ask you. She'll be glad I've found an old friend to go with."

"Old friend?" Daisy echoed.

"You know what I mean. So," he went on briskly, "Saturday night. Black tie. The equivalent for you. I'll pick you up a little before eight. Where do you live?"

"What? No! Wait. I didn't agree."

"So you don't stand behind your own advice?"

Daisy opened her mouth to object, and couldn't find words to convince herself, let alone ones that would convince as stubborn a man as Alex.

"I can't," she said feebly.

"Why not?"

Because I don't have a babysitter. She didn't say that, even though it was certainly true. "I— My wardrobe doesn't run to that sort of thing."

"Get something suitable," he directed. "I'll pay for it."

"You will not. I can't—"

"Did you or did you not tell me to take my time, get to know Caroline?"

"Yes, but—" She stopped, waiting for him to cut her off, but he didn't. He waited in silence for her next reason she couldn't go. And she didn't have one—other than self-protection.

Maybe she was protesting too much. Maybe going with him would be the best self-protection there could be.

Maybe spending an evening with Alexandros Antonides, going on a date with him, would actually force her to "move on" once and for all.

Last time she'd felt like Cinderella going to the ball—and she'd believed she'd found Prince

Charming. If she went now, she would go with no illusions at all.

She could even dance with him—but know it ended there—know that her happy ending was waiting at home in her life with her son.

She would be in no danger of succumbing to airy-fairy fantasies. She would enjoy the evening and come home at midnight—unlike Cinderella—with both shoes on and her heart intact.

Daisy took a breath. "Yes, all right. I'll do it."

"Great." He sounded pleased. "What's your address?"

"I'll meet you there."

Alex argued. Daisy was adamant. He said she was being silly. She said she didn't care.

"I'm not your real date. I don't need to act like one. I will see myself to the Plaza and I'll see myself home afterward."

"Daisy, that's ridic—"

"Take it or leave it."

There was a long silence, then an exasperated sigh. "Fine. Quarter to eight. Front steps of the Plaza. This Saturday. Don't be late."

She was out of her mind.

Absolutely insane.

She couldn't go out with Alex! She didn't have

a babysitter. And even if she could find one, she didn't have a dress. Nor did she have a fairy god-mother and some talented singing mice who could whip one up in an afternoon.

She was in a complete dither the next afternoon when Izzy and the boys stopped by for a visit after Rip's orthodontist appointment.

Izzy took one look at Daisy pacing around the kitchen and demanded, "What's the matter with you?" Her boys went running out back to play with Charlie, but Izzy stood right where she was and studied Daisy with concern.

"Nothing's wrong with me."

"Really?" Izzy's tone dripped disbelief. "You're pacing the floor. You're tearing your hair."

True, but Daisy stopped long enough to put the kettle on. "I have to go out tomorrow night. To the Plaza."

Izzy's eyes widened. "A date? At last!" She beamed and rubbed her hands together.

"Not a date! Nothing like that," Daisy said quickly. "It's business. Well, sort of business." She couldn't quite explain.

"Who with?" Izzy demanded.

"A cousin of Lukas's. An old…friend." Which was the truth, wasn't it? Alex had even called her "an old friend." "I knew him years ago. He's interested in getting married. Wanted me to match-make for him. I said no. Now he's got a serious girlfriend, but she's out of town. So he asked me to go in her place."

It sounded quite believable to Daisy.

Izzy immediately caught the snag. "Why wouldn't you matchmake for him? I thought you loved matching people with their soul mates."

"Yes, but—" She wasn't going into what Alex thought about soul mates. "I didn't feel I knew him well enough." Daisy turned away and started rearranging the forks in her silverware drawer. A Tarzan-like yodel from the backyard turned her around in time to see Izzy's oldest son, Rip, hurtle out of the tree at the end of the garden. He and his younger brother, Crash, were Charlie's heroes.

"Mountain goats," Izzy muttered. "I can make them stop if you want."

Daisy shook her head, grateful the conversation had veered away from Alex. "It's all right. Charlie loves trying to keep up with them. And it's good for him to have them. He needs older brothers."

"Not these two." Izzy winced as Crash followed his brother's leap with one of his own. "What's he like? This cousin of Lukas's," Izzy elaborated at Daisy's blank stare. "Your 'old friend'? One of the dark handsome Antonides men, is he?"

Daisy did her best at a negligent shrug. "I guess."

"Not a wild man like Lukas, I hope."

"No. He's not like Lukas," she said. "He's very... driven."

"Is that why you're chewing your nails?"

"I'm chewing my nails because I can't find a babysitter. I already called your girls."

"Tansy and Pansy are hopeless now they're in college," Izzy agreed cheerfully. "They have lives." She sighed. "But no worries. I'll keep him."

Daisy blinked. "You will? Are you sure?"

"Absolutely. If you don't mind me having him at our place." Izzy picked up the kettle and began pouring boiling water because Daisy wasn't doing it. "He can even spend the night. In case you don't want to turn into a pumpkin right after the Plaza." She grinned.

Daisy flushed and shook her head. "Not a chance. I am a pumpkin. Home before midnight. This is not a date. But Charlie would love to go to your place, if you're sure."

Izzy waved a hand airily. "I'll never notice he's there." She zeroed back in. "What are you wearing?"

"That's my other problem," Daisy admitted. Nothing in her wardrobe lent itself to upscale fundraisers at the Plaza. And despite his brusque "Get something. I'll pay for it," she had no intention of allowing herself to feel beholden to Alex.

Izzy was thoughtfully silent for a long moment. Then, "I might have something," she said, looking Daisy up and down assessingly. "Ichiro Sorrento," she said.

"What?"

"That new designer whose collection Finn shot last year. Japanese-Italian. You remember him?"

Daisy did. But she shook her head. "No way I can afford anything with his label."

"You don't have to. You can wear mine. Remember that gorgeous dress and jacket I wore to Finn's opening last spring?"

Daisy's eyes widened. "*That* dress?" The dress had been a deep-sapphire-blue silk, spare and elegant, with an exquisitely embroidered jacket in the same deep blues, emerald-green and hints of violet. "You don't want me wearing your gorgeous dress. I'd spill something on it."

"I already have. It doesn't show," Izzy said cheerfully.

"I'm taller than you are."

"Everyone is taller than I am," Izzy countered. "So what? You'll just show more leg. I doubt anyone will mind. Especially—" she grinned "—not a male Antonides."

"Not. A. Date," Daisy reiterated firmly. "I'm not trying to show off my legs."

"Of course not. But you're not a nun, either. You need to knock Mr. Driven Antonides's socks off. Make him forget all about his serious girlfriend and run off to Vegas with you!"

It was as if a little devil called Izzy was sitting on her shoulder tempting her. "Dream on," Daisy scoffed.

"A little dreaming never hurt anyone," Izzy retorted.

Daisy let her have the last word.

But in her heart she begged to differ.

Where the hell was she?

Dozens of hired cars and limos and taxis slid up to the Plaza's entrance Saturday evening while Alex stood on the steps, shifting from one foot to the other, watching and waiting. There were snowflakes in the air. Alex could see his breath, and his shoulders were getting damp as the snow melted, but he couldn't bring himself to go inside and wait and pace.

There were scores of black-tie-clad men and elegantly dressed women getting out of taxis and limos—and not one of them was Daisy.

He'd told her quarter to eight. It was almost ten

after. He'd got here early, to be sure he was here when she arrived, and she was nowhere to be seen.

He should never have given in to her demand that she come on her own, that he neither pick her up nor take her home after. He'd agreed only because she would have refused to come otherwise. The sweet and malleable Daisy he had known five years ago might still be somewhere inside this Daisy Connolly, but he hadn't caught a glimpse of her in a long, long time.

Was this her revenge? Was standing him up payback for his having said he wasn't interested in marriage all those years ago?

He shouldn't have asked her to come. It was a damn fool idea. When Caroline had said she couldn't make it, but suggested he invite his friend Daisy, he'd been surprised.

"My friend Daisy?" he'd echoed, puzzled.

Caroline had shrugged. "I assume she's your friend. You talk about her all the time."

Did he? Surely not. But he could hardly deny their friendship if it came across that way to Caroline because how could he justify talking about her if she wasn't a friend? What would Caroline think if he said she wasn't a friend at all, she was...a thorn in his side, an itch he never quite managed to get rid of. Like poison ivy, perhaps.

So he'd shrugged and told Caroline he'd ask. And, hell, why not? He could prove to Daisy that he'd listened, that he hadn't gone straight home and asked Caroline to marry him. He'd done what Daisy suggested and got to know her.

He hadn't fallen in love with her. That wasn't going to happen. He knew it. Caroline knew it.

They had seen each other as often as their schedules allowed. They always had a good time. Relationship-wise they were on the same page—and perfectly happy to be there. And if they still hadn't managed to make it to bed together, well, the time had never been right.

She'd had an early meeting or he was flying off to Paris. She was in Rio or he was in Vancouver. It had nothing to do with memories of Daisy in his bed. She hadn't been in this bed.

Only in his bedroom. And the fact that he couldn't forget that was still driving him nuts.

"Alex!" A hearty booming voice from the doorway startled him back to the present—back to the lack of Daisy anywhere in sight. He turned to see Tom Holcomb, the hospital's vice president in charge of building development.

Tom was grinning broadly, holding out a hand to shake. "Good to see you. Big night for you."

He pumped Alex's hand, then looked around. "Where's your date?"

Alex opened his mouth, hoping that a suitable polite reply would come out when, all of a sudden, from behind a hand caught his.

"Sorry," Daisy said, catching her breath.

Alex turned his head, saw her smiling up at him, and felt his heart do some sort of triple axel in his chest. There was a glow to her cheeks, as if she'd been running, but she was smiling.

And so was he. His heart which, after the triple axel, had seemed to stop all together as he looked at her, began beating again. "About time," he said gruffly, swallowing his relief. She was gorgeous. She wore a long black wool dress coat and he could barely get a glimpse of the dress beneath it, but what he could see seemed to sparkle—just as Daisy did. Her eyes were alight, electric almost, taking in everything. She'd pinned her hair up in some sort of intricate knot which reminded him of the way she'd worn it at the wedding when he'd met her. He remembered taking it down, running his fingers through it. Felt a quickening in his body at the temptation to do it again now. It was, after all, already slightly askew, as if she had been running.

"My cab got stuck in traffic. Think I stood you up?" She laughed.

"No." He wiped damp palms down the sides of his trousers. He wasn't admitting anything.

"Your date, I presume?"

Alex was suddenly conscious of Tom Holcomb still standing beside him, looking with interest at Daisy.

Alex nodded and drew her forward. "This is Daisy Connolly. Daisy, Tom Holcomb. He is the VP in charge of building development, the man I worked with on the hospital design."

"The man who rubber-stamped his terrific ideas," Tom corrected, shaking the hand Daisy offered. "I'm delighted to meet you. Are you an architect, too?"

"No. A photographer," Daisy said, shaking the hand he held out. "I recently did a photo shoot of Alex at a building he restored in Brooklyn."

"A man of many talents," Tom agreed. He drew Daisy with him into the hotel, asking questions about her own work which she answered, still smiling. And Daisy, with a glance back at Alex, went with him.

Alex stood watching, bemused, and somehow a little dazed.

Dazed by Daisy. Dazzling Daisy, he thought, smiling wryly at his own foolishness. But it was true. And he didn't mind following, it gave him a chance to admire her from another angle.

From any angle tonight she was elegant, sophisticated, tailored, stylish. She would never be the stunning classical beauty that Caroline was. Daisy's nose still had a spattering of freckles, her cheekbones were not quite as sharply pronounced. Her mouth was less sculpted than impish. And you could never say that Daisy had every hair in place.

But everything about her was alive—from her unruly hair to her lively sparkling eyes to her kissable lips.

Alex tried not to think about her kissable lips. It wasn't as if he was going to be tasting them again this evening. Furthermore, he reminded himself, he shouldn't even want to. He was this close to buying Caroline an engagement ring.

But Caroline's kisses had never intoxicated him. They'd never made him hot and hard and hungry in a matter of an instant. He'd lost every bit of his common sense that weekend with Daisy—and she hadn't had any at all.

There had never been anything cool, calm and collected about her. She was a lead-with-her-heart, damn-the-torpedoes, full-speed-ahead sort of woman.

Basically the anti-Caroline. And Caroline was what he wanted.

Wasn't she?

"Are you coming?"

Alex jerked his brain back into gear to see that Tom had disappeared into the hotel, but that Daisy was still standing at the top of the stairs by the revolving door, waiting.

"Got distracted. Sorry." He bounded up the steps, feeling awkward, caught out. And feeling that way, he challenged her. "Been running?" he asked her gruffly.

"I told you," she said with some asperity. "The cab was caught in traffic. I left it in the middle of Columbus Circle."

"You *walked* from Columbus Circle?" Wide-eyed he stared at her high pointy-toed heels.

"No," she said flatly. "I ran."

Definitely the anti-Caroline. Alex shook his head, dazed and amazed, and unable to keep from grinning. "Of course you did."

Daisy glared, her eyes flashing. "You said not to be late!"

"So I did." His grin widened briefly, then he met her gaze. "Thank you."

Their eyes locked. And Alex felt the electricity arc between them exactly the way it always did.

It didn't seem to matter that she was all wrong for him. He jerked his gaze away from hers, but it only went as far as her lips. Nervously she licked them.

Alex's body went on full alert.

Daisy tore her gaze away. "It sounded like the sort of occasion where it wouldn't do to waltz in late," she said, a little ragged edge to her voice. "Not if you're at the head table."

She was right, of course. He was being a fool—again.

Impatient with his own weakness, Alex gestured her brusquely into the revolving door. "Well, let's not waste your sacrifice, then. We'll go in."

Daisy was in complete control.

She might as well have had a squadron of singing mice and a fairy godmother the way everything had fallen into place. Izzy was keeping Charlie, the glitzy shimmery dress fit perfectly, the sophisticated black dress coat her mother had given her for her birthday was beautifully appropriate. Other than the stupid traffic jam and having to run quarter of a mile and that she could feel her hair slipping from its knot, she didn't have a care in the world.

Granted her first glimpse of Alex in formal attire, complete with black tie, pristine white shirt, checking his watch impatiently as he waited for her, had made her mouth dry and her heart gallop. But, Daisy assured herself, that was because she'd just been running, not because of the man himself.

Still, once in the hotel, on the arm of the handsomest man in the room, it was hard not to believe she was channeling Cinderella.

Daisy had been to the Plaza before. But she'd never been to An Event.

This was An Event—in a cavernous room that despite its immensity, managed somehow to seem warm and appealing and elegant with matte gold walls, burgundy drapes, glimmering sconces and crystal chandeliers. The dozens of tables wore pristine white damask linens, sported napkins folded by origami experts, and had settings of gleaming china and rows of delicate stemware.

Not a bowl of mac and cheese in sight.

When she worked for Finn, Daisy had gone to plenty of glitz-and-glamour events. In the fashion industry they'd been brasher and flashier, not to mention, thousands of decibels louder than this one. A girl from small town Colorado had been very much out of her league. But after the first half dozen or so, she had become blasé and soon she began waltzing through them without batting an eyelash.

Of course those rarely required her to look suave and elegant and remember which fork to use. Tonight there looked to be a surfeit of forks. But it wasn't the number of forks that was making her blood race. It was Alex.

"Can I get you something to drink? Wine? A cocktail?"

"I'll have a glass of wine," Daisy decided. "Red."

They'd drunk a smooth dark burgundy when they'd first met. If she was going to rewrite the ending of their encounter, she would begin tonight the way they'd begun before. But this time she wouldn't let herself embroider the circumstances with airy-fairy fantasies of happily ever afters.

"Burgundy," Alex said, surprising her. Did he remember? But she couldn't—wouldn't—ask.

"I'll be right back." He headed toward the bar.

When he returned, drinks in hand, Daisy was standing near the wall right where Alex had left her. She drew his eye clear across the room. The dress he'd glimpsed before she'd shed her coat definitely lived up to its promise. Its blue-green iridescence sparkled like northern lights as it molded her every curve. The short embroidered jacket covered more than he wished, hinting at bare shoulders beneath, smooth shoulders he remembered kissing all too well.

But it was more than the dress that drew his gaze, more than the dress that made the woman. There was a warmth and a vibrant energy in Daisy—as if she were the only person there in three dimensions. Everyone else seemed flat by comparison.

She had been alone when he'd left her, but now she was chatting with hospital CEO Douglas Standish and his wife. Daisy's expression was animated, interested. He remembered her that way from the moment he'd first seen her. She engaged with people, drew them out. She had drawn him.

Never particularly social, Alex had attended the wedding with the intent of leaving as soon as it was reasonable to do so. He'd drifted around the periphery of the room, keeping his eye on the exit—until he'd seen Daisy.

Then he'd only had eyes for her. It was still that way.

Now he wound his way through the crowds of people, heading toward her as determinedly as he had that long-ago day.

"Here you go." He handed the drink to Daisy, then turned to Standish's wife. "May I get you a drink?"

"No, thank you, dear. Douglas will do that. I just wanted to meet your lovely lady—and tell her how lovely you are—" her eyes twinkled merrily when

Alex opened his mouth to protest "—and what an amazing gift you've given us with the design for the hospital wing."

"Thank you for saying so."

She patted him on the sleeve. "Have a wonderful evening. You deserve it. So nice to meet you, dear," she said to Daisy, before taking her husband's arm and guiding them into the crowd.

"So," Daisy said, looking him in the eye when the other woman had left, "you're the guest of honor. And you couldn't be bothered to tell me?"

Alex shrugged. "It's no big deal."

Daisy's eyes glittered. "It's a huge deal," she contradicted him. "Huge. Apparently your hospital wing has broken new ground in patient services. It's celebrated worldwide." She had gone beyond glitter to glare now. "They're giving you an award."

"I told you that when you did the photos for the article."

"An award, you said. You didn't tell me anything about it. It might have been for perfect attendance at meetings for all I knew! This is wonderful!" And now her wonderful eyes sparkled with warmth and delight, and in spite of himself, Alex felt a rush of pleasure. "Did you tell Caroline?"

"No," he said, surprised.

"Why not?"

He shrugged. "It's nothing to do with her."

"Of course it is!"

Baffled, he shook his head. "Why?" She hadn't done anything. He hadn't even known her when he'd done it himself.

"Because *you* did it! Because you're her man."

But he *wasn't* Caroline's man. He wasn't anyone's man. But he wasn't going to have that argument with Daisy now. Fortunately people were beginning to head to their seats. So he just said, "Come on. We need to go sit down." He took her arm, more aware of touching her than he was whenever he touched Caroline. He led her to the table where they would be sitting, then pulled out her chair.

Daisy flounced down into it, but she still wasn't done. She looked up at him, her expression annoyed. "She'd be thrilled," she told him. "And proud. I am—proud," she said, "and it's nothing at all to do with me."

Alex felt a warm flush of pleasure at her admitting that. What he didn't do was tell her that it wasn't entirely true.

He would never have taken the commission at all if something she'd said to him hadn't stuck with him for the past five years. Initially he'd said no.

He had no interest in hospital design. He didn't like hospitals. Hated them, in fact.

After his brother had got leukemia, Alex had spent far too much time in hospitals watching his brother suffer and become more and more remote. It had devastated him. Even now Alex associated hospitals with the most painful period of his life.

After Vass's death, Alex had never set foot in one again. Even when he broke his arm playing lacrosse in college, he'd insisted on having it set at a doctor's office. "No hospital," he'd said firmly. It was the last place he wanted to be.

He didn't talk about hospitals, either. Didn't talk about Vass. Never had to anyone. Except that weekend when Daisy had got under his skin.

He supposed it was because she was just getting her equilibrium back after losing her father. Barely fifty, he'd been born with a heart defect that had grown worse over time. He'd been in and out of the hospital often, she'd said. And the sad wistful look on her face had prompted Alex to confide that he, too, hated hospitals.

"They take away your life," he'd said harshly, remembering how remote and sterile they had seemed, how they'd isolated his brother, how Vass had wanted to come home so badly, to be out, to be anywhere but there. "They don't save it."

He'd expected her to agree.

Instead she'd shaken her head. "It wasn't the hospital's fault. Without the care my dad got there, we'd have lost him sooner. But it was hard for him to feel connected. He felt so isolated, like he wasn't really a part of things anymore."

Vass had said the same thing.

"There was only one window," she'd gone on. "But he couldn't see outside from his bed. So we used to pretend. We'd close our eyes and pretend he was home or we were going fishing in the San Juan or even doing chores, chopping wood for the fireplace. He loved that fireplace..." Daisy had swallowed then, and her eyes had glistened with unshed tears. She'd blinked them back rapidly. "It wasn't the hospital's fault," she repeated. "But it could have been better. It could have been more."

Her words had made Alex think.

What if Vass had had a chance to spend time in a hospital that had allowed him to feel connected. What if he'd been able to do, at least virtually, the things he wanted to do—like go back to the beach near their island home, or drive a race car, or sail over the Alps in a hot-air balloon?

Once Alex opened the floodgates, the ideas wouldn't stop coming. And what hadn't been possible twenty-five to thirty years ago was within reach now.

Alex's hospital wing was full of windows—floor-to-ceiling in many rooms. Even treatment rooms, wherever possible, brought the outside in. If a patient wanted to see the world beyond the walls, he could. The semirural setting just across the river north of the city provided views of the countryside as well as the city skyline. And it wasn't just about the visuals. Alex worked in sound systems and even olfactory ones, connecting senses to the world beyond the hospital's confines.

He had provided virtual worlds, as well. Patients in the wing he'd designed could close their eyes as Daisy's father had, but they could also use modern electronics to create the sights, sounds and smells of the seashore, the woods, the inside of a race car or the ballroom of a fairy-tale palace.

He told her about it now, aware of the way she looked at him, as if he could hang the moon. The salads that had been in front of them when they'd sat down remained virtually untouched.

"It sounds like an amazing place." Daisy smiled, a smile that went all the way to her eyes, that touched—as it always did—a place hidden somewhere deep inside him that no one ever reached but her.

He cleared his throat. "If you have to be in a hospital," he agreed gruffly, "if you can't have what the rest of the world takes for granted, I guess it will do."

Their eyes met. And Alex knew that whether or not he mentioned his brother or her father, Daisy remembered. Daisy knew.

What surprised him, though, was her withdrawal. One minute she'd been gazing at him with warmth and admiration. The next some shadow seemed to settle over her, her expression shuttered.

"I'm sure that all the children will appreciate it." Her tone was polite, but she seemed suddenly more remote. She turned to her salad and began to eat.

Alex was more nettled by her withdrawal than he would have liked. But really, what difference did it make? He hadn't done it for her. He'd done it for people like her father, his brother. He dug into his own salad.

Neither of them spoke until the salads were taken away and the entree was set before them. Then Daisy turned toward him again. "What sort of building are you working on now?"

So they were going to be polite and proper and distant. Fine by him. Alex was glad to talk about the present so he told her about the office building he was designing on the edge of Paris.

Daisy had never been to Paris. And as he talked, he saw her eyes begin to sparkle again. Her remoteness vanished. Her questions came more quickly, and her enthusiasm was contagious. He wanted to make her smile, wanted to have her cock her head and listen eagerly. Alex found himself telling her not just about his work in Paris, but about the city itself, about places he liked, things he'd seen, galleries he visited, buildings he admired.

"You used to live there, didn't you?" It was the first time she'd alluded to the past.

"Yes. And then I was here for a while. But I went back four or five years ago," he said. He knew precisely when he'd gone—and why. After the disastrous end to his weekend with Daisy, New York had more memories than he wanted. Paris seemed like a far safer place to be.

It was only in the past six months or so—when he'd made up his mind to marry, in fact—that he'd returned to live more or less permanently in New York. Even now, though, he kept his small flat in the fifth arrondissement.

Their talk moved from Paris to the Riviera, to other places he'd been. Daisy asked about all of them. The women Amalie had set him up with had asked questions, too, but not like Daisy. Not as if they cared about the answers.

Daisy did. And her interest and enthusiasm drew him out. He would have liked to show her Paris, to walk the wide boulevards and narrow lanes with her, to sit at a tiny table in an outdoor café and drink strong dark coffee with her, to wander through the museums and the galleries hand in hand with her, to walk along the Seine with her and kiss her there, to run through a rainstorm with her.

To take her back to his little garret flat and make love with her. He could imagine Daisy there, letting him strip off her little embroidered jacket, then letting him find the zip at the back of her dress and lower it slowly. He'd kiss his way down—inch by luscious inch and—

"And what?" Daisy was looking at him, curious and impatient.

Hot. God, he was hot. And hard. And suddenly aware that he was in the middle of a crowded room with the object of his fantasy studying him worriedly. Her eyes were still bright and eager, but she was looking at him with puzzlement.

"What happened? You stopped talking," Daisy said. "Did you just get distracted?"

Alex's heart was still hammering, his body still feeling the effects of what he'd been thinking about—her. He shifted in his chair and cleared his throat. "I did, yes." He gave a quick shake of his head. "Sorry about that."

He didn't let it happen again, even though he was still intensely aware of her. It was almost a relief when dinner ended. Except then the speeches began, and Alex knew he would have to say something when the award was presented.

Public speaking wasn't his forte. He preferred to speak with his work, with his design, with his buildings, not his words.

But when the time came, Daisy clapped madly and beamed at him encouragingly when Douglas Standish beckoned him to the podium to accept his award.

Alex made it brief. He gripped the podium and stared into the bright lights as he thanked the hospital board who had given him the opportunity to design the wing and the committee who had given him the award. It was what he had prepared, and it was all he had intended to say.

But before he could walk away, his gaze slid across the hundreds of people in the room and, looking down, he didn't see the lights. He saw Daisy.

His mouth went dry at the sight of her upturned face, at her avid expression, her tantalizing smile.

And he didn't walk away. He looked at her, spoke to her.

His voice was less stilted and more ragged as he said, "I hope this wing makes a difference to the patients. I hope it gives them the safe haven they need to get well and—" he paused, his eyes still locked with hers "—the connections to the world outside to keep them strong."

Like your father never had. Like my brother never had. And you're the only one who knows why I did it.

He could see that in her eyes, the realization dawning, her lips parting in a silent O.

Alex jerked his gaze away and abruptly shut his mouth. Then, clutching the award in a sweaty hand, he said hoarsely, "Thank you all," and strode back to his chair and sat down.

His heart was crashing in his chest. He didn't look at Daisy. He didn't have to. He could sense her eyes on him. The awareness, the emotion vibrated between them. So damn much emotion it felt like being swept off by a tidal wave. He kept his gaze resolutely on the platform where Douglas was coming back to speak.

With a few brief words he thanked Alex again, then thanked all the hospital's staff and benefactors for their support. Then the doors opened to the adjoining ballroom and the small live orchestra just beyond those doors began to play.

People stood up, couples headed toward the dance floor. Alex breathed again.

Abruptly he stood and held out a hand. "Let's dance."

CHAPTER SEVEN

PUTTING her hand in his was like touching a live wire.

A current of electricity seemed to flow between them, one even stronger than the flickering awareness she'd felt all night.

Daisy was aware of the pressure of Alex's strong fingers wrapping around hers as he led her through the doors and onto the dance floor. But it was nothing compared to her awareness when he took her in his arms.

She almost stumbled against him as she tried to do the opposite and keep a respectable distance between them. It was a battle because every instinct in her went to him like a moth to the proverbial flame.

Every touch was memorable. His fingers encased hers warmly. She was exquisitely aware of his hand pressing lightly at the small of her back. She was close enough that she could catch a faint hint of soap and aftershave. And a quick glance showed her how smooth-shaven his jaw was. She remembered it rougher, had loved to stroke her hand over it, stubbled one way, smooth the other.

Abruptly she turned her head, trying to follow his lead at the same time and nearly tripped over his foot. He caught her, pulled her closer. And Daisy knew the sensation of her body melting into his, as if she belonged there, wrapped in his arms.

She had danced with lots of other men. She had felt other men's hands on her body. None—not even Cal's—evoked such strong reactions.

Even now, knowing he was not for her, knowing for a fact that she and Alex had no future, Daisy could not deny that Alex's touch, Alex's smile, Alex's gaze brought to life something inside her that no other man's ever had.

Dancing with Alex was, just as it had been five years ago, the Cinderella experience that Daisy had remembered.

She understood now how she had been swept away by it. There was a feeling of rightness, of perfect understanding, that she'd never had with anyone else. And it scared her to feel it again and know how wrong it had been.

She forced herself to remain clearheaded and sane. She looked away from his hard jaw to study the room, determined to commit it to memory. She focused on the music, tried to think of the title, the composer, to isolate the instruments. And all the while she was aware of the man who held her in his arms.

His breath teased the tendrils of her hair. His trouser-clad legs brushed the silk of her dress. And every touch, every brush set off a hum of something electric. And the study of the room and the music and everything else faded away.

It was all right, she told herself. Nothing was going to happen on a dance floor. He couldn't sweep her off her feet. She couldn't slide a hand between the buttons of his shirt.

So where was the harm in appreciating the feel of hard muscles under her fingertips? Why not give in, just for the moment, to the instinctive rhythm they seemed to engage in when they moved to the music? As long as she didn't allow herself to remember the instinctive rhythm they'd brought to their lovemaking…

There was a point beyond which lay foolishness. Daisy had been there once. Never again.

Careful, she warned herself. Be careful.

But her head turned and so did his. Her lips brushed his jaw. His touched her ear. A shiver ran from the hairs on her neck to the tips of her toes. Her body trembled. Her knees wobbled. And deep in the center of her, something ached with the desire she refused to admit.

She took a breath. "So," she said, "tell me about Caroline."

She was gratified when Alex seemed briefly to stumble. But then he caught himself and without even looking directly at him, she saw his jaw ease as if he were smiling.

"Caroline is amazing," he said. "She's quick. Witty. Beautiful."

His voice was warm, animated. Of course it was. Caroline was his woman. *Remember that,* Daisy told herself sharply and kept asking him Caroline-related questions.

Maybe it was masochistic. Maybe it was just the only way to keep her common sense. Whatever it was, it helped. Daisy made herself listen as he told her all about the ad campaign Caroline was developing that had taken her to Hong Kong. Alex told her about how Caroline had been headhunted by five different companies in the past two years.

"She's amazingly successful. Definitely making her mark. She's even thinking she might go out on her own in the next couple of years." He clearly approved of her ambition and her talent. Daisy forced herself to think about that and not about the way his legs brushed against hers.

"So what are you waiting for if she's so wonderful?" She ventured a glance at his face, wanting to see his expression.

A tiny crease appeared between his brows. The muscles in his shoulder tensed beneath her hand, and hard green eyes looked down into hers. "I thought you weren't in favor of quick decisions these days," he said sharply.

"Yes, well, I'm not you."

Alex grunted. He didn't say anything else. Didn't answer. Didn't talk about Caroline anymore, either.

Daisy tried to stifle her irritation. She told herself it didn't matter, but for some reason it did. It would be easier if he were engaged. Easier to stop thinking about how damned appealing he still was.

Well, fine, if he wouldn't help her out by talking about Caroline, she'd talk about the pulmonologist whose photos she'd taken for Lauren Nicols.

"I have to thank you for sending Lauren my way," she said. She didn't really want to be beholden to him. But it was her own work that had caused Lauren to call, nothing he'd done. So she talked about that. And Alex seemed grateful enough to take up that topic of conversation. Then the dance was over, and Douglas Standish asked to partner her for the next one.

She danced with half a dozen men, and only reaffirmed that no one's touch affected her the way Alex's did. She seemed to be aware of him—where he was, who he was dancing with—even when he was nowhere near. Actually though, he always seemed to be somewhere fairly near. Wherever her partners danced her, Alex was never far away.

She tried not to look at him, tried not to envy the women he held in his arms, tried not to gauge if he had held them as closely as he'd held her. But she couldn't help noticing that while he danced and chatted with them, his gaze often sought her.

It didn't mean anything. It couldn't.

But she couldn't quite stifle the gratification she felt every time she felt his eyes on her. She didn't dare catch his eye, though. It would be playing with fire. And Daisy had no intention of playing with fire, though there seemed to be one kindling somewhere just south of her midsection, and every time she looked his way, the fire grew.

The evening passed quickly. It was nine-thirty. Ten. Then nearly eleven. They danced. They visited with people Alex had worked with. They danced again. And this time the flames burned even hotter than before.

His eyes seemed to bore into hers whenever she looked at him. Their legs brushed. Their bodies touched. Against her breasts, she could feel the beat of his heart. With everyone else they spoke easily, casually. But when they danced, they had little to say to each other, and the conflagration continued to build.

It wasn't yet midnight, not even eleven-thirty. But Daisy knew she needed to be sensible. While she wouldn't turn into a pumpkin at midnight, and Izzy was keeping Charlie until the morning, a woman could stand just so much temptation.

But one more dance wouldn't hurt, she thought as the music began again and, wordlessly, Alex drew her once more into his arms. They hadn't danced with each other two dances in a row. But it seemed natural now. Right.

Inevitable.

Just as, inevitably, in a few minutes she would say thank-you for a nice evening and take her leave.

But now—just for a few moments more, Daisy allowed herself the luxury of lingering close to him, to luxuriate in the warmth and the nearness of his body, to relish the shiver she felt at his warm breath against her hair.

It's all right, she assured herself. It's just now. Just this moment. Not forever. She had no expectations this time. She was only making memories that would last her through the years.

Her body trembled. Vibrated. Particularly her hip.

Her hip? For a moment she didn't know what was happening. The vibration stopped, thank God. But almost instantly, it started again.

Daisy stumbled, realizing that this vibration had nothing to do with the nearness of Alex and everything to do with the tiny mobile phone she'd tucked into the on-seam pocket of the dress.

"You won't need it," Izzy had said.

But Daisy had insisted. Most glitzy high-fashion dresses clung so tightly that anything more than underwear—and sometimes even that—was too much. But Izzy's gorgeous kicky swirly dress flared at the hips, and Daisy had put her phone into one of its tiny pockets.

"Just in case," she'd said, patting it.

"Suit yourself. I won't be calling you," Izzy had vowed.

But someone was calling her now.

Alex caught her when she stumbled. "What's wrong?"

"It's my phone."

His brows drew together. "Your *phone*? Who the hell do you need to talk to tonight?"

Daisy didn't answer that. "Sorry." She shrugged, half apologetic, half worried as she slipped out of his arms and moved to the edge of the dance floor. "I have to get this."

Alex followed her. "One of your clients out on a hot date and need advice?" he growled.

Daisy glanced at the caller ID. It was Izzy. She answered at once. "Is it Charlie? What happened? What's wrong?"

"He's fine," Izzy said quickly. She sounded as out of breath as Daisy felt. "Well, not entirely fine. But nothing life-threatening. Really. Don't panic."

"What *happened*?" Daisy pressed the phone hard against her ear, trying to hear above the music.

"He was following Rip," Izzy reported ruefully. "Doing what the big boys do. They were climbing on the bunk beds. Rip has this notion that he can move all around their bedroom without touching the floor—"

"Oh, God."

"Well, he can," Izzy admitted. "Of course he's bigger than Charlie. He has longer arms and legs. More wingspan."

Daisy didn't need to have it spelled out. "Oh, God," she said again, knees wobbling.

"Charlie's a pretty impressive climber," Izzy said with the calm that came from having got sons through the first decade of their adventurous lives. "And jumper—but he didn't quite make it to the top of the chair from Rip's bunk. He's broken his arm. I'm so sorry, Daisy. I feel terrible. I—"

"Where is he? St. Luke's?"

"Yes. Finn's taking him. We're on a first-name basis with the emergency room staff."

"I'll meet him there." Daisy was already headed for the nearest exit so she could grab her coat and then a cab.

"I'm so sorry," Izzy repeated. "And Rip is devastated."

"Tell him not to worry. I'm sure it will be fine." She just needed to get there. Now.

"I feel so responsible. Or, as Finn says, irresponsible."

"Don't. It's not your fault."

"It is. I forget how much younger Charlie is. Call me as soon as you've seen him. Promise?"

"I promise." Daisy stuffed the phone back into her pocket and headed for the cloak room.

"What is it? What happened?"

Dear God, she'd forgotten about Alex!

Daisy shot him a quick glance and apologetic smile over her shoulder. "I— It's…an emergency. A friend…" She gave a vague wave of her hand as she skirted around groups of people in the foyer. "I'm sorry. I have to go."

"I figured that out," Alex said gruffly. "Not a client."

"No."

"Your ex?" he bit out.

Daisy blinked at him. "What?"

"Guess not. A new boyfriend?" His gaze narrowed. When she didn't answer, it narrowed further. "Did you tell him you were coming out with me?"

There were no answers to anything he was likely to ask now. "I need to go, Alex," she repeated, then forced herself to stop and face him squarely, even managing to paste a smile on her face. "Thank you for this evening. I enjoyed it."

"I did, too," he said, a grim set to his mouth. Then he stepped around her to present the claim check for her coat to the lady behind the desk.

"Thank you. You don't have to wait. I'll just catch a cab."

He didn't reply. But he didn't leave, either. And moments later, when the lady brought her coat and she reached for it, Alex was there first, shaking it out and holding it so she could slip it on.

"Thank you." As the coat settled on her shoulders, Daisy flicked a grateful smile in his general direction. "I'm sorry to run off. I did have a lovely evening." She paused, hoping he'd say, *Of course,*

I understand. Thank you for coming. Then, nice-ties observed, she could dart away.

He said, "I'll come with you."

"No! I mean, no, thank you. It's not necessary. Really, Alex. I mean it," she said when she saw his jaw tighten. "Thank you for everything, but I'll say good-night here." There was a moment's silence. Then, not knowing what else to do, she thrust out a hand for him to shake.

He looked at it as if she'd offered him a poison-ous snake.

Hastily Daisy withdrew it. "Good night, Alex." And without giving him time to reply she turned and darted out of the hotel to catch a cab.

He should just let her walk away and get on with his life.

It was clearly what she wanted. Whatever the hell she was doing, dropping everything and run-ning off at the drop of a hat, it wasn't any of his business.

Alex knew that.

She didn't want him there. He knew that, too.

But he couldn't let her go and face whatever the hell she was about to face when the mere thought of it turned her white-faced and stricken.

So what if it was a boyfriend? Once he saw that

she was all right, he'd leave her to it. To him—the boyfriend. Though he couldn't help grinding his teeth at the thought.

The cab he'd grabbed outside the Plaza took a right on Fifty-seventh and headed west. It was Saturday night in midtown, and the traffic was bumper-to-bumper traffic. The theaters had just disgorged people by the hundreds onto the streets. Progress was excruciatingly slow.

He should have just followed her straight out the door. But she'd got a head start on him, and then Standish had called his name. There was no way to pretend he hadn't heard, and impossible to be impolite and brush the older man off—not without being able to offer a convincing excuse.

And what was he going to say? "My date had to rush to the hospital because she thinks her ex-husband…or maybe her boyfriend…or some guy she knows called Charlie needs her?"

Damn it. Didn't she have any pride?

He glared out at the traffic, willing it to move. At least Standish had told him where St. Luke's was. It wasn't that close to Daisy's office, though perhaps it was near where she actually lived.

He didn't even *know* where she lived. Something else she hadn't shared with him. And something else to fume about until the driver dropped him off outside the emergency services department and sped away.

Facing it, Alex's feet suddenly felt rooted to the pavement.

He didn't do hospitals. Of course he'd been in and out of the hospital he'd designed the wing for. But he'd never been in it other than for work. He'd never been in a hospital for anything resembling a medical reason—for anyone—since the day Vass died. Everything in him wanted to walk away.

Only the memory of Daisy's stricken face made him take a breath, then another deep one, and stride straight in.

It was a zoo. There were people everywhere, sitting, standing, crying, bleeding, filling out forms.

Not one of them was Daisy.

Alex stood by the door, cracking his knuckles. He didn't even know who to ask for. Charlie Somebody.

Hell, he didn't even know the guy's last name. He got in line anyway. Maybe he'd spot her before he had to come up with a name.

He was two cases from the desk when he heard the sound of her voice. His head jerked around, his heart lurched at the sight of her drawn pale face.

She stood in the doorway of one of the examining rooms, her expression intent as she listened to a white-coated doctor. Whatever he said, she nodded, still looking fragile. The doctor patted her arm, then went into the room. Daisy started to go after him.

Alex went after her. "Daisy!"

She jerked as if she'd been shot. Then she spun around, white as a sheet.

He started to go to her, but instead she hurried toward him. "What are you doing here?" Her voice was thready, strained.

He just looked at her. "You're here."

She swallowed. Something shuttered in her gaze. "You don't need to be here."

"You look like hell."

"Thank you so much."

He moved closer. She moved back until he'd cornered her between a chair and the wall. Then he put a hand on her arm so she couldn't pull away. "I came to see if I could help, Daisy."

She shook her head almost fiercely. "I don't need your help. I told you that. It'll be all right."

"Charlie will," he clarified, needing to see her reaction to his name. He tried to keep his voice even, nonjudgmental, but he didn't like it when she flinched.

Her jaw tightened. Her fingers knotted.

"Is it bad?" he asked. He didn't want the guy to

die, for heaven's sake. He just didn't want Daisy dropping everything to race across the city for him.

"He has a broken arm."

"A broken arm?" Alex almost laughed with relief at the same time he felt a surge of annoyance. "All this hysteria for a broken arm?"

"I'm not hysterical!" Daisy said indignantly. There was color in her cheeks again.

He couldn't help grinning. "No? Taking a phone call in the middle of a dance? Rushing out of the hotel? For a broken arm?"

"I apologized," Daisy said tightly. She hugged her arms across her chest. "You didn't have to come. I certainly didn't invite you!"

"I thought he might be dying. You looked devastated. I didn't want you to have to face it alone."

Something flickered across her features. She hesitated for a moment, as if she was giving him the benefit of the doubt. Then she nodded. "That was kind of you. Thank you. But it really wasn't necessary." She straightened, pulled her arm out of his grasp, and gave him what he supposed was a dismissive smile. "It will be fine. *He* will be. I just… Maybe I overreacted. Don't worry. No one's going to die. Now, please excuse me." She tried to slip around him.

But Alex was in no mood to be dismissed and he blocked her way. "Who is he, Daisy?"

She didn't answer. He didn't think she was going to. But then a nurse poked her head out of the examination room. "Mrs. Connolly, Charlie's asking for you. Doctor is going to put the cast on now."

Once more Daisy started to move away, but Alex caught her arm. "He's *asking* for you?" he said mockingly. "To what? Hold his hand?"

Her teeth came together. Her eyes flashed. "Maybe. He's a little boy," she snapped, her eyes flashing anger. "He's my son."

Her *son*? Daisy had a *son*?

But before he could do more than reel at her words, Daisy had jerked her arm away, cut around him and stalked back into the examination room. The door shut behind her with a resounding bang.

A dozen people stopped talking and looked around in surprise.

Alex felt as if he'd been punched. *Where the hell did she get a son?*

Well, of course, he supposed she'd got the boy the time-honored way—she and her ex. But why hadn't she mentioned him?

Not that it was his business. But still…

Alex glared at all the people who were still murmuring and staring at him as if it were his fault she'd stormed away and slammed the door. He wouldn't have minded slamming one or two himself. Instead he stalked over to an empty chair by the windows and flung himself down.

He didn't know how long he waited. Long enough to have plenty of second thoughts. Daisy wasn't going to be happy to come out and find that he had waited. She'd made that perfectly clear.

And did he really want to meet Daisy's child?

It was annoying enough to think that she had professed to love him, then turned around and married someone else. To be honest, Alex had felt a certain satisfaction knowing her rebound marriage hadn't lasted.

That it had resulted in a child was somehow disconcerting.

A child. Charlie.

Alex tried to imagine a little boy who looked like Daisy. Would he have her mischievous grin, a dimple in one cheek, freckles across his nose and a mop of honey-colored hair?

Or would the boy look like her ex-husband? Was the ex holding Charlie's other hand in the exam room with them now? Alex straightened in the chair, scowling at the thought.

Maybe he was going to be sitting here when all

three of them came out of the room together. And wouldn't that be awkward as hell?

The noise of a crying baby, a croupy cough, a parent and teenager arguing washed right over him. Alex paid no attention. So it would be awkward. So what? He'd walked out on her and their child, hadn't he?

Alex almost hoped the S.O.B. was here. He'd like to see what was so wonderful that Daisy had ever married him. Scowling, he shifted irritably in the chair, then looked up to see Daisy coming out of the examining room.

On her hip was a little boy with a mop of brownish-blonde hair and one arm in a bright blue cast. He'd expected a two- or three-year-old. But this boy looked bigger. Alex leaned forward, studying him intently. But he couldn't see much. There were people in the way.

Daisy was listening to the nurse. They were standing just outside the exam room door. The boy was listening, too. Then he turned his head to look out at the waiting room.

Alex's breath caught. His heart seemed to stutter even as he stared.

Charlie's jaw was squarer than Daisy's, his lower lip fuller, his nose a little sharper, his cheekbones higher. His eyes weren't blue, they were green.

He didn't really resemble Daisy at all. Even his hair was actually a deeper gold than Daisy's. But Alex knew exactly who he was. He had known another boy with those eyes, that jaw, whose hair had been exactly that color.

His brother. Vassilios.

CHAPTER EIGHT

FOR a moment Alex couldn't move. Couldn't think. Could only stare.

And understand the implication. It hit him like a fist to the gut.

He moved on automatic pilot, putting himself between Daisy and the door. And all the while, he couldn't take his eyes off the child.

The boy was Vass all over again. Alex's heart squeezed in his chest. His throat tightened. He couldn't swallow. He barely had a toehold on his composure when Daisy finished talking to the nurse and turned—and saw him.

She stopped, rooted right where she was.

Their eyes locked and he watched her color fade. Her lips parted and trembled. Her arms tightened around the boy in her arms and she glanced around as if looking for another way out.

Bad luck, Daze, Alex thought grimly. Nowhere to go but through me.

She understood that, for a second later she

straightened her shoulders, lifted her chin and walked straight toward him.

"I told you that you didn't need to wait."

Alex felt a muscle in his temple tick. He swallowed, seeking words. There were none. Only a well of pain.

How could you? His eyes asked her. The boy—his son!—was close enough to reach out and touch.

He balled his fingers into fists, every fiber of his being wanted to reach out to the little boy, to take him in his arms and never let him go. But the boy didn't know, wouldn't understand. Even Daisy seemed to think he was behaving oddly.

"Are you all right?" she asked when he didn't reply.

She had no idea. Didn't realize what he knew. Of course, she wouldn't. She had no idea Charlie could've been Vass's clone. Alex managed a curt nod. "Fine." Poleaxed, in truth.

"Good." She smiled briefly. "It was kind of you to bother," she said. "But not necessary."

It was necessary. Alex knew that down to his toes. He just looked at her. For a moment neither of them spoke, neither moved.

"Mommy."

Daisy shifted at the sound of the small plaintive

voice. She hugged the little boy close. "This is Charlie," she said. "Charlie, this is Mr. Antonides."

Your father.

God, how he wanted to say the words. He didn't. He just studied the boy up close. His cheeks were fuller than Vass's had been. But at that age, maybe his brother had had round cheeks, too. Alex would have been too young to recall. But Charlie had the same freckles across his nose that Vass had had, the same long lashes.

"I got a brok'n arm," the boy told him in a froggy little voice.

Alex nodded and met his chocolate gaze. "Yeah, I see that you do."

Daisy shifted under the boy's weight. "I need to get him home. Thank you. I'm sorry that the evening ended this way."

I'm not. Alex didn't say that, either. He dragged his gaze away from the boy long enough to meet hers. It all made sense now—her distance, her coolness, her determination to shut him out.

But he wasn't out any longer—and he had no intention of ever being out of this child's life again.

"Come on," he said. "Let's get you into a cab." He stepped back to let Daisy go through the door. It was late, well after midnight, and the snow was still falling. Charlie couldn't put his arm in his jacket, and Daisy was trying to pull it more closely around his shoulders.

"Let me." Alex took the boy's puffy red down jacket and settled it around small bony shoulders. His hands trembled as he brushed them over him, then tucked the jacket close between Charlie's body and his mother's. "There you go." Even to his own ears, his voice sounded hoarse.

"Thank you." Daisy flicked him a quick smile.

There were no taxis right outside. So he strode off to the corner to flag one down. He half expected Daisy to have vanished by the time he got back with it. But sanity must have prevailed. Either that or she was too shattered by the events of the evening to pull a disappearing act.

Alex opened the door to the taxi. "After you. I'll take him." He held out his arms.

"I can manage." She tried to get in with the boy in her arms, but she nearly lost her balance, and Alex scooped him away.

And the moment the boy's solid body settled in his arms, Alex felt something in him change. Something strong and protective took root, dug in. Instinctively he moved his face closer to the boy's soft hair, drawing in the scent of antiseptic, bubble-gum shampoo, laundry soap and earthy little boy.

His breath caught, his grip tightened.

"I can take him now." Daisy's hollow-eyed gaze locked with Alex's as she held out her arms to the little boy.

Slowly, carefully—reluctantly—Alex settled him on the seat next to her. Then, not giving her a chance to tell him he didn't need to come along, he slid into the backseat as well and shut the door.

There was silence except for the taxi's public service babbling. The car didn't move.

"You'll have to tell him where we're going," Alex said at last. "I don't know."

Daisy hesitated for a split second, then in a low voice gave the cab driver the address. It was the same address as her office.

As the cab lurched forward, he narrowed his gaze at her. Daisy kept hers focused straight ahead. Charlie huddled between them. Alex could feel the little boy's bony shoulder pressed against his arm. He angled his gaze down to see the top of the boy's head, the burnished gold of his hair, the sharp little nose and what looked like a stubborn chin. Looking at him, Alex felt his throat tighten with so many emotions he couldn't name them all.

Charlie.

His son.

Alex turned the notion over in his mind. Tested it. Tasted it. Wrapped his entire being around it.

Then he lifted his gaze and looked over the top of Charlie's head at the woman who hadn't even bothered to tell him and felt his whole body stiffen with anger.

As if he were aware of something wrong, Charlie stiffened, too. He edged closer under his mother's arm.

Was he scared? Certainly he sensed something was amiss. Kids could do that, Alex remembered. He certainly had.

He'd read his parents' body language for years. He had sensed their worry about Vass, even when they'd tried to say everything would be fine. He'd felt their pain, their hurt at his brother's illness. He'd felt, without needing words, their emotional withdrawal.

He didn't blame them. His brother had been his idol. His hero. He knew as well as they had that Vass was the best person in the world. And he instinctively felt what they felt: that if they had to lose one of their sons, it should not have been Vass.

Moody, temperamental, fidgety, less-than-perfect Alex was the one who should have died.

Of course no one said so. No one had to. Kids could read body language. They could hear the feelings in the silences—as Charlie could no doubt hear his now.

Consciously Alex relaxed his body and stopped glaring at Daisy. Instead he shifted slightly away so that he could look down at Charlie more easily.

"I'm not Mr. Antonides. I'm Alex," he said.

The boy flicked a quick glance up at him and dipped his head in acknowledgment.

"Want to shake left hands?" Alex asked.

Charlie's gaze lifted again to meet his. Alex could feel Daisy's eyes on him, as well. Wary, suspicious. Charlie hesitated a moment, then nodded and stuck out his left hand. Small fingers gripped his.

And Alex knew that this first mutual touch was momentous, and that the feel of that small warm hand in his was a memory he would carry with him to his grave.

"I broke my arm once, too," he told the boy, "when I was ten."

"Did you jump off a bunk bed?"

So that was what Charlie had done. Alex smiled and shook his head. "I was climbing some cliffs. One crumbled and I fell."

If he had been on the cliffs near their Santorini home, he didn't think it would have happened. He knew those cliffs like he knew the inside of his bedroom. He and Vass had climbed them their whole lives.

But they hadn't been in Santorini. They had been at a place they were renting in Athens while Vass was in the hospital for treatments. Alex had hated it there, hated the hospital, hated the house, hated having to play by himself all the time because Vass was too ill to do anything.

And he'd only made things worse when he fell.

"You don't think!" his mother had raged. "You never think!"

"You should be glad it hurts," his father had said sternly. "Maybe you will not be so inconsiderate again."

"I wish I'd been with you," Vass had whispered when Alex finally got to see him. His brother's eyes had had dark circles under them. But they had still glittered with urgency and desire.

And Alex had said fervently, "Me, too."

Now, trying to push aside the painful memory, he smiled at the little boy who was looking up at him with Vass's eyes. "Did you break yours jumping from a bunk?"

"I was tryin' to get to the dresser like Rip does."

"Who's Rip?" Whoever he was, Alex liked his name.

"One of Finn and Izzy MacCauley's boys," Daisy said. "Rip is Charlie's hero. He tries to do whatever Rip does, in this case, apparently, to get around the house without touching the floor," she said despairingly.

Alex grinned. "I used to do that, too."

Charlie's eyes widened. "You did?"

"It's something all boys do?" Daisy looked dismayed.

"It's a challenge," Alex told her. "Boys like challenges. How old is Rip?"

"Almost twelve," Daisy said. They were speeding down Central Park West. There was little traffic now and they were hitting the lights. It would be a matter of minutes until they were at Daisy's office.

"That explains it," Alex told the little boy. "You've just got to get bigger."

"Mom says I can't do it again."

Daisy looked mulish. "I don't want him killing himself."

"He won't," Alex said. He smiled at Charlie. "You look like a pretty tough guy."

The boy's head bobbed. "I am. My dad says so."

"Your dad?" Alex lifted his gaze to look from Charlie to Daisy. "His dad?" he said to her.

"His dad." Daisy's look was even more mulish and her tone even firmer than before. "My ex-husband. Cal."

Alex's jaw tightened at the lie. He stared at her.

And just as if she were telling God's own truth, Daisy stared defiantly back. Their gazes were still locked when the cab turned the corner on Daisy's street and pulled up midblock in front of her place. He understood it was more than her office now. She damned well lived here, too.

"Here's where we get out," Daisy said briskly. She reached into the pocket of her coat and pulled out money for the cab.

"I'm paying," Alex said flatly.

Daisy opened her mouth as if to protest, but then shrugged. "Thank you."

He paid the driver, then opened the door and got out, reaching back in and lifting Charlie carefully up into his arms, settling him against his hip. Charlie looped an arm over his shoulder.

Daisy scrambled out and looked disconcerted to see the boy in Alex's arms and not standing on the sidewalk where she had apparently expected to see him.

Alex nodded toward the building. "After you."

He wasn't surprised when Daisy fished a key out of her pocket and, instead of going up the stoop, led the way through a wrought-iron gate and down the steps to the door below. Her movements were jerky as she fumbled the key, but finally unlocked the outer door and pushed it open, then did the same with the lock on the front door, and turned to hold out her arms for her son.

Still carrying Charlie, Alex pushed straight past her into a tiny foyer filled with jackets and boots and roller skates and the smallest bicycle he'd ever seen.

"Yours?" he asked Charlie.

The boy's head nodded against Alex's shoulder.

"Can you ride it?"

Another nod, this one firmer than the last.

"Good for you. I had a bike when I was your age." Alex smiled. Bikes had been his thing—never Vass's. And already Charlie rode one. So there was that bit of himself in his son. "We'll have to go riding."

"He has a broken arm," Daisy said sharply.

"Not now." Alex turned and faced her. "There will be time." He watched that register in her brain before he said to Charlie, "Plenty of time."

"Alex," Daisy protested faintly.

He turned his stare back on her until her gaze slid away.

"You got a bike?" Charlie asked, interested.

"Yep. I race bikes."

Charlie looked fascinated. Daisy looked dismayed. She shook her head, as if resisting everything. Then quickly and deliberately she stripped off her coat and hung it on one of the hooks in the foyer and crossed the room, holding out her arms.

"Give him to me. He needs to get ready for bed. Now."

Alex wanted to argue. Wanted to defy her, hang on to his son. But for all that he was furious with Daisy, none of it was Charlie's fault. But his jaw was tight, his whole body felt rigid as he loosed his grip and eased the boy into his mother's arms. He took special care not to jar Charlie's arm. And once he'd let go, he smoothed a hand over Charlie's hair, letting it linger.

"You're a brave guy," he said, keeping his gaze on Charlie.

The boy nodded solemnly.

"We'll ride bikes together sometime soon," Alex promised, his smile crooked. "Okay?"

Another nod and a tentative smile.

He could hear Daisy's indrawn breath. "Good night, Alex." She paused, then added evenly, "Thank you for…everything."

For everything? His eyes asked her.

For giving you a son?

"Who's he?" Charlie asked as Daisy carried him up the stairs.

"A man I used to know. A…friend." But she was

distracted as she spoke, remembering Alex's narrowed gaze as he'd watched her carrying Charlie across the emergency room.

He didn't know, she assured herself. He couldn't.

It was Charlie's mere existence that had surprised him—that *she* had a son. And his terseness simply meant that he was annoyed she hadn't told him.

In Charlie's room, she flicked on the light and deposited him gently on the bed. She rarely carried him anywhere these days, and having done so now, she was almost out of breath, surprised at how big he'd gotten since she used to carry him all the time.

"My arm hurts."

"I know. I'm sorry." She bent to kiss his soft hair, then smoothed her hand over it, pulling back as she remembered that Alex had just done the same thing. "I guess maybe you won't leap from bunk beds anymore?"

Charlie pursed his lips, considering. "Not till I'm bigger," he decided. "Crash can do it."

"Maybe you should wait till you're nine or ten then." She got his pajamas off the hook behind the door.

"Maybe." Charlie took the pajamas, then tried

to wriggle out of the jacket he still had over his shoulders and one arm.

"I'll help you tonight," Daisy said. "But you're going to have to figure out how to do it yourself, too." She eased off the jacket, then lifted the hem of his shirt and began to slide it up and over his good arm and his head.

"Maybe Alex could teach me."

"What?" She jerked back, then stared at the pair of bright eyes that popped into view as the shirt came off. "Why would he?"

"'Cause he broke his arm," Charlie said simply. "He'd know how."

"Oh. Well…" Daisy made a noncommittal sound. "I'm pretty sure you can figure it out without Alex's help." She finished getting his clothes off and his pajamas on. "Go wash your face and brush your teeth."

Charlie flopped back on the bed. "But I'm tired. Do I hafta?"

"Yes. Even boys who fall off bunk beds have to maintain a minimum of civil decorum."

"I didn't fall," Charlie protested. But he allowed her to pull him up. "I jumped. An' what's 'civil deck-somethin'?" Charlie loved big words.

"Civil decorum," Daisy repeated. It was what she had tried to maintain for the past hour and a half. She said, "Behaving like a well-brought-up *clean* child."

"Ugh." But Charlie slid off the bed and padded toward the bathroom while Daisy gathered up his clothes. "Oh!" she heard him say brightly. "Hi."

"Hi." The unexpected sound of Alex's voice right outside the door sent Daisy hurrying out. She skidded to a halt a second before she collided with his chest.

"You didn't leave."

"No." He had propped a shoulder against the wall outside Charlie's bedroom door and stood there meeting her gaze, then his eyes dropped to Charlie, and Daisy felt more than a flicker of unease.

He didn't say anything. But even quiet and unmoving, his presence seemed to overpower everything else. He was too big. Too close. The space was too intimate. And the situation didn't bear thinking about. She didn't want him here.

But she didn't know how to get rid of him without causing Charlie to wonder what was going on. He already had to wonder. No man but Cal had ever been upstairs.

But Alex was, right here in the hallway, his dark hair disheveled, as if he had run his fingers through it. He looked incongruous here in his formal evening wear, but even as she thought it, she realized the formal evening wear wasn't so formal anymore. He'd removed his tie—it dangled from his pocket—and he'd undone the top two buttons of his shirt.

It had the effect of making him look more masculine and primal than ever—with the added misfortune of reminding her of how he'd looked five years ago when she'd brought him into her tiny apartment after the wedding. He was all the things he'd been then and all the things she'd been at pains to resist earlier this evening—too broad-shouldered, too imposing and too damned predatorily male.

"I came to say good night to Charlie." His tone was measured, his words easy, understandable and, to Charlie, unthreatening.

But Daisy knew a threat when she heard one. She took a quick breath. "Say good night, Charlie."

Charlie tipped his head back to look up at Alex, but instead of saying good night, he said, "Can you teach me to get my shirt on an' off over my cast?"

Alex nodded. "I can."

"No, he can't. It's after one in the morning. You need to go to bed," Daisy said firmly.

"I'll show you," Alex promised smoothly. "Tomorrow."

"But—" Charlie began.

"Your mother's right," Alex said firmly. "You need to sleep."

"I can't sleep. My arm hurts," Charlie argued.

"But you're tough," Alex reminded him. The two of them looked at each other. Two men understanding each other—even though one of them was only four.

"Teeth, Charlie," Daisy said firmly. "And wash your face. Now." She took hold of his shoulders and steered him past Alex, doing her best not to brush against him in the narrow hallway. If she'd hoped he'd take the hint and go, she was out of luck.

He didn't budge, just waited until Charlie had brushed his teeth—awkwardly because he had to do it left-handed—and scrubbed at his face with a washcloth. He didn't use soap, but Daisy didn't make him do it again. She just wanted him in bed.

"Right," she said briskly. "Off to bed."

Obediently Charlie headed back down the hall, but stopped directly in front of Alex. He looked up again. "G'night."

And Daisy remembered when she'd seen the photo of Charlie looking up at Cal's father and had realized how similar her son's profile was to Alex's. They were indeed remarkably alike.

Was that how Alex had known? Or was it some

scary primal innate recognition between father and son? She didn't know. She only knew that the still-deep emotion that she could sense simmering in Alex was more elemental than just a response to discovering she had a child she hadn't told him about.

The question was no longer: *Did he know?*

The question was: *What was he going to do now?*

He reached out a hand and brushed the top of Charlie's head once more. "Good night," he said gravely. "It was nice meeting you, Charlie." His fingers lingered for a moment, then he withdrew them and tucked them into the pocket of his trousers and brought his gaze up to meet Daisy's. "At last."

She suppressed a shiver, then swallowed. With her eyes she beseeched him to be silent, and was relieved when he didn't say anything else. Giving him a fleeting grateful smile, she slipped past him to follow Charlie into his bedroom where she shut the door with a solid click.

Whatever Alex might have to say to her—and she had no doubt he had plenty to say—he could say it tomorrow. Or next month. Not now.

Her priority was Charlie. It was the middle of the night and he'd been hurt, and it didn't matter that her brain was whirling a million miles a minute. If she pushed him, he would balk and take even longer.

So she did everything in his bedtime routine. She tucked him in, then read him a bedtime story. She listened as he told her about his day, including a long involved account of everything he'd done at Rip and Crash's house, what he didn't like about the emergency room, and ultimately, as she'd feared, questions about Alex.

"Do you think he'll ride bikes with me?"

"I don't know," she said. "He's a busy man."

"He said he would."

"Yes. And maybe he will."

"Remind him."

Daisy made a noncommittal sound. "Prayers," she reminded him, and when he'd finished, she added a desperate silent one of her own. Then she kissed her son good-night.

Charlie clutched her hand when she got up to leave. "Stay."

"Charlie."

"My arm hurts. Sing to me," he pleaded.

That wasn't part of the regular nightly routine, but sometimes when he was sick and irritable, she could calm him with some silly songs. "You're tired."

His big eyes drooped even as he nodded. "I'll sleep. Sing."

So Daisy turned out the light, determinedly shut out the turmoil roiling around in her mind, and sat back down on the bed beside him.

Maybe it would soothe them both, she thought as she began to sing. There was a boat song, and a campfire song, and a bus, train and truck song. She had made them up about Charlie's life when he was a toddler. He knew them by heart. Now he settled against her, his eyes shut, the blue cast dark against the pale blanket that covered him. His breathing slowed.

Her voice slowed, too, and finally stopped. Waited. Watched him. And finally when she was sure he was asleep, she dipped her head and kissed him.

"I love you," she whispered, brushing a hand over his hair. Then she put out the bedside light and slipped quietly out of his room, shutting the door after her.

The clock in her bedroom said five minutes of two. Daisy felt as if she'd been up for two days. Or weeks.

Wearily, she stripped off Izzy's dress. It still sparkled in the soft bedside light. It had made her sparkle in the beginning. She didn't sparkle now. She felt as if she'd been run over by a truck. She flexed her bare shoulders and shivered as she stared into the mirror over her dresser. A pale, hollow-eyed, haunted version of herself stared back.

She felt ill. Exhausted. And scared.

Alex knew. And soon he would confront her about Charlie. He would say whatever he had to say about the son he hadn't known he had. The son he never wanted. She felt a tremor run through her.

Whatever he said, he could say it to her. He wasn't going to say it to Charlie. Charlie wasn't ever going to hear that he wasn't wanted. Ever!

Maybe, with luck, Alex would pretend he didn't know. Maybe he would simply walk away. She could hope.

Quickly pulling on her nightgown, she wrapped up in her fuzzy chenille robe and tiptoed down the hall to brush her teeth and wash her face. Then she went downstairs to let Murphy out. She would have done it when she first got home, but Charlie had taken precedence.

Murphy wagged his tail, delighted to see her. She rubbed his ears and kissed the top of his head. Then she slid open the door to the back garden, Murphy went out, and she slid it closed against the snowy December night. Then, while he was out there, she went to put the dead bolt on the front door. Alex couldn't have done it when he left.

If he had left.

He hadn't. He was sprawled, eyes closed, on the sofa.

CHAPTER NINE

FOR a moment Daisy didn't even breathe, just pressed a hand protectively against her breasts and felt her heart pound wildly beneath it.

She dared hope he was asleep—because hoping he was a figment of her imagination was not a possibility. But even as she did so, Alex's eyes fluttered open and he rolled to a sitting position.

"What are you doing here?" she asked.

Alex rolled his shoulders, working the stiffness out. He had taken off his coat and the stark white of his shirt made his shoulders seem broader than ever. He looked at her levelly. "Waiting for you."

"It's late!"

His eyes bored into her. "Five years late."

"I don't know what you mean," she said. Her fingers knotted together.

"You know." His gaze was steady, his eyes chips of green ice.

"Alex," she protested.

"We're done playing games, Daisy."

"I'm not—"

"We're going to talk." There was a thread of steel in his voice now, and as he spoke, he stood up. Slightly more than six feet of whipcord muscle and testosterone somehow filled the room.

Daisy stepped back. "I have to let the dog in."

He shrugged. "Go ahead. I'm not going anywhere."

Exactly what she was afraid of. She hurried through the kitchen and fumbled with shaking fingers to open the sliding-glass door for Murphy. It wasn't just her fingers shaking, her whole body was trembling, and it had nothing to do with the cold December night. The cold in Alex's stare was a different story.

Murphy trotted in, wagging his tail cheerfully. Daisy shut the door and slid the bolt home, then cast a longing look at the stairs that led up to her room. But retreat wasn't an option. So, wiping damp palms down the sides of her robe, she went back to the living room.

Alex was standing by the mantel, holding the photo of her and Charlie and Cal taken last Christmas. At her footsteps, he took one last look and he set it back on the mantel, then looked over at her. "Is this your ex?"

She nodded. "That's Cal."

"Very cozy."

"It was Christmas. Christmas is cozy."

"You look happy."

"We were happy." She hugged her arms across her chest.

"You were still married to him then?"

"No."

One dark brow arched in surprise. "But you had a picture taken together?"

"Yes." She wasn't giving him any explanations. She didn't owe him any.

"He's not Charlie's father."

"Yes, he is." She had been married to Cal when Charlie was born. He was the father on Charlie's birth certificate. He was the father that Charlie called Dad. He was a father to Charlie in every way that mattered.

"Not by blood, he's not."

Daisy swallowed, then lifted her chin. "And you know this how?"

He reached into his back pocket and pulled out a thin black leather billfold. Opening the wallet, he took out a photo, crossed the room and handed it to her. It was a small color snapshot of two young boys, grinning at the camera.

Daisy saw only one. He could have been Charlie. He was older than Charlie, maybe nine or ten.

But his eyes were Charlie's—the same shape, the same light color. He had the same sharp nose, spattered with freckles, the same wide grin. He even had the same straight honey-blonde hair that she'd always assured herself had come from her side of the family.

She clutched the photo so tightly, her fingers trembled. Her throat tightened and she shut her eyes. She couldn't breathe.

Alex didn't seem to be breathing, either. He was stone silent and unmoving. Waiting for her to speak?

But what could she say?

Slowly she opened her eyes again and began to study the picture more carefully. The two boys were standing on a beach, bare-chested and wearing shorts, the sea lapping bright blue behind them. They had their arms slung around each other's shoulders and they were laughing into the camera. The older boy was the one who looked like Charlie. The other was younger, maybe six or seven, with a front tooth missing. He had dark shaggy hair and light eyes. Daisy knew those eyes.

Slowly, cautiously, she looked up at them now. "It's you…" she said so softly she doubted he could hear her. Her thumb stroked over the dark-haired boy's face. "And your brother."

A muscle ticked in his jaw. He nodded. "Vassilios."

Of course it was. His beloved brother, his hero, the beautiful loving boy whose death had destroyed his family looked almost exactly like Charlie.

Dear God, what a shock seeing his son must have been.

Outside a siren wailed as a fire truck went up Central Park West. Inside, the room was so silent she could hear the old oak mantel clock tick. She could hear Murphy two rooms away in the kitchen lapping up water. It was the calm before the storm.

"Why the hell didn't you tell me?" His voice accused her, anguished, ragged, furious. He plucked the photo back out of her hand, his fingers fumbling as he slid it back in his wallet and shoved it into his pocket.

She heard the pain, the anguish, the accusation. On one level she understood them. But she remembered pain and anguish of her own.

"Why the hell should I?" she countered, stung by his fury. "You didn't want a child. You said so! I babbled about marriage and family and you were quite clear. No marriage. No family! Why should I have told you?"

"That was before I knew I had one! How could I

say I didn't want my son when I didn't even know he existed?"

"You didn't want him to exist!"

His nostrils flared and his jaw clamped shut. He balled his fingers into fists, as if he were trying to control what he did with them. Like strangle her. "You kept my son from me!"

"I took you at your word!"

"Damn it!" Alex let out a harsh breath. He glared at her, then raked his fingers through his hair and paced the room. At the far end, he whirled around. "You knew how I felt about my brother!"

Yes, she had known. She knew that Vassilios had been the favorite son, the star, the heir. She knew that everyone had loved him. Even Alex. Especially Alex. Vassilios had been bright, funny, caring, social. Everything, Alex had told Daisy five years ago, that he himself was not.

But Vass had been so wonderful that Alex hadn't envied him. He'd only wanted to be like him. He had loved his brother deeply. Vassilios's death had irrevocably changed his life.

She had known that losing his brother was the main reason Alex never wanted children. It was the reason Alex had originally never wanted to marry. He didn't want to love, he'd told her. Love hurt.

Dear God, she could agree with that. She'd hurt

more in the aftermath of his leaving and her discovering she was having his child than she could ever have imagined. She'd loved him—and lost him—and for nearly five years now had Charlie to remind her of that loss.

But she couldn't regret it. She couldn't even regret marrying Cal. At least they'd had some sort of love. They'd tried.

Alex had refused to even try. Not then. Not now. He still wanted a marriage on his terms, a marriage without love. And children had still been a deal breaker. He'd made that clear.

So now she met his accusation squarely and told him the honest truth. "Yes, I knew," she agreed. "But mostly I knew you didn't want children. I did what I had to do. I did the best that I could for my son."

"Really? And you and dear Cal have such a spectacular marriage." His tone mocked her, infuriated her.

Daisy had to fight her own inclination to look away. Even so she felt her face heat. "Cal is a great father."

"And I wouldn't have been?" His challenge was loud and clear. Mostly loud.

"Not if you didn't love him! And be quiet. You'll wake him up."

Alex's teeth came together with a snap. She could hear his harsh breathing, but he didn't claim he would love Charlie. How could he? He'd already hardened his heart.

"Why would I think you'd be a good father to a child you didn't want?" she said. "Cal was. Cal was there when he was born—"

"Because you damned well didn't tell me!"

"Cal loves him," she finished quietly.

"And I've never had a chance to!"

"You didn't want one. You'd already made your choice. And when I found out I was pregnant, I had to make choices, too. I chose to do what I thought was best for Charlie. He needed love. He needed parents. A family. You didn't want that. You said, 'No entanglements, no hostages of fortune.'"

He had actually used those terms, and when she repeated them now, she saw him wince. "You said love hurt too much. You wanted nothing to do with it."

They glared at each other. Daisy wrapped her arms across her chest and stared unblinkingly at him. She knew what he had said, and Alex would be lying if he denied it now.

He didn't deny it. He didn't say anything at all. His jaw worked. His eyes reflected his inner turmoil. Seconds passed. Daisy could hear Murphy's toenails clicking down the hallway as he came out from the kitchen to look at them inquiringly.

Alex didn't notice. He was cracking his knuckles, then kneading the muscles at the back of his neck. He paced the room like an agitated animal trapped in a cage. Finally he flung himself down on the sofa and rubbed his hair until it stuck up all over his head. He dragged his palms down his face and stared at her bleakly over the top of them. "Hell."

In a word, yes.

It was a hell she was already familiar with. The confusion, the anguish, the damned-if-you-do, damned-if-you-don't choices she had faced when she'd discovered she was pregnant. She remembered the hollowness she'd felt at Alex's flat-out rejection of any sort of relationship. In the face of her hopes and dreams and—let's face it—fantasies, he had been crystal clear.

She hadn't even wanted to imagine what he would have said if she'd turned up on his doorstep and announced she was expecting his child. The very thought had made her blood run cold. Even now she shivered inside the thick robe she was wearing. Tucking her hands inside the opposite sleeves, she chaffed her arms briskly, trying to warm them.

Alex just sat there. He didn't speak. He didn't move, except for the rise and fall of his chest. His expression was grim as he stared across the room. He wasn't looking at her now.

She wondered what he was seeing in his mind's eye. His dying brother? His unknown son? The parents who had rejected him and each other? His life, as carefully designed as any building he'd ever planned, going down the drain?

She couldn't imagine. Didn't want to.

Murphy stood between them, looking from one to the other as if wondering what they were doing in his living room in the middle of the night. Finally, accepting it as dogs always did, he curled up on his bed in front of the fireplace and put his head between his paws.

Alex looked up and met her gaze. "I want my son."

"Want your...?" Daisy stared at him, breathless, as if he had punched her in the gut. "What does that mean? You can't take him!" she blurted, anguished. "You don't have any right!"

"I didn't say I was going to take him." Icy green eyes collided with hers. "But I'm not walking away, either."

Daisy swallowed, tried to think, to fathom what

Alex's "not walking away" meant. For Charlie. For her. She didn't have a clue.

She only knew what she must not let happen. "You're not hurting him," she said fiercely. "I won't let you."

Alex rubbed a hand over his hair. His brows drew down. "Why the hell would I want to hurt him?"

Daisy had started to pace, but she stopped and turned to face him. "I didn't say you would intend to. But it could happen. He's only four, Alex. He won't understand. Besides, he has a father."

Alex's jaw tightened. "Cal." He spat her ex-husband's name. "Did you marry him because of Charlie?"

Daisy ran her tongue over her lips as she tried to decide how to answer it, how to be honest and fair to both Alex and to Cal.

"Did you?" Alex persisted when she didn't reply.

She sat down in the armchair across from the sofa where he was leaning toward her, his elbows on his knees, his fingers laced. "Yes," she admitted. "But it wasn't as simple as that. I didn't go find the nearest eligible man and ask him to marry me."

"No?" He mocked her.

Daisy tried not to bristle. "No," she said firmly. "Cal asked me."

"And you jumped at it."

In fact she'd been shocked. It had never occurred to her. They'd been friends. Nothing more. "I thought about it. He insisted we could make it work."

"Sounds passionate," Alex drawled.

"Cal and I had been friends for a long time. He said love wasn't just a matter of passion. It was a matter of choice. I thought he was right. He wasn't. But—" she met his mockery defiantly "—I love Cal."

"You thought you loved me."

"I did," Daisy agreed. "But that was before I found out you didn't give a damn."

Alex stiffened as if she'd slapped him, then surged to his feet and loomed over her. "So you fell out of love with me and in love with What's His Face in, what? Six weeks? Less?"

"It wasn't like that."

"No? So, what was it like?"

She knew he didn't really want to hear the answer. He was angry and he just wanted to put her on the defensive, pick a fight.

But Daisy wasn't buying into that. "Sit down," she said, and pointed at the sofa when he didn't move. "Sit down and I'll tell you what it was like," she repeated sharply.

His gaze narrowed on her, but when she kept pointing, he dropped onto the sofa, still staring at her unblinkingly.

When he had settled again, Daisy tucked her feet under her and tried to find words that would make him understand.

"I was hurt when you didn't feel what I did that weekend," she began.

Alex started to interrupt, but she held up a hand to stop him. "I know you think I shouldn't have been. You think I presumed too much, And—" she took a steadying breath "—you were right. I presumed far too much. But I was young and foolish, and nothing like that had ever happened to me before."

Alex's mouth was a thin line, but he was listening at least.

Daisy twisted the tie of her bathrobe between her fingers, staring at it before lifting her gaze again. She shrugged and told him helplessly, "I fell in love with you. It was a mistake, I admit that." She laced her fingers in her lap and dropped her gaze to stare at them. If she looked at him, she'd realize that she was actually saying these things—and she didn't want to be saying any of them.

She wanted her life back—the way it had been before she had gone to the dinner with him tonight, the way it had been before everything she'd worked so hard to build and hold together for the past five years had all come apart at the seams.

"When you walked out, I was humiliated," she said. "I felt like an idiot. Sick."

Alex's jaw bunched. She knew he wanted to argue. He shifted uncomfortably. Daisy didn't care. She was uncomfortable, too. They could suffer through this together.

"Weeks went by," she continued. "Two, three, four—and instead of being able to put it behind me, I just felt sicker. And sicker. I started throwing up every morning. And that," she said, lifting her eyes to look at him squarely now, "was when I realized that it wasn't the memory of my idiocy that was making me sick. It was being pregnant."

He flinched, then let out a slow breath.

"I didn't even think about trying to find you," she said levelly. "You'd made it quite clear you weren't interested in any sort of involvement at all."

"You could've —"

"No," she said flatly. "I couldn't." She hesitated, then just told him the truth. "I was afraid you might want me to get an abortion."

He stared at her, shocked. "How could you think—?"

"Why wouldn't I?" she demanded. "You didn't want to care! I was afraid you'd say, 'Get rid of it before *anyone* cares.' Well, *I* cared. Even then I cared!" She could feel tears stinging the back of her eyes.

"Jesus," he muttered.

"Exactly," Daisy said, understanding the desperation that made him say it. "I did a lot of praying. You can believe that. I was scared. I didn't know how I was going to cope. I could keep working for Finn while I was pregnant, but after the baby came, I thought I might have to go back to Colorado and stay with my mother till I could work something out. And then—" she breathed deeply "—Cal proposed."

"Your savior. He was just standing around, waiting in the wings, for exactly that moment?" Alex demanded bitterly. "Ready to take some other man's woman?" Alex ground out. "His *pregnant* woman?"

"I was *not* your woman! And he was my friend. He *is* my friend."

"And yet you couldn't stay married to him," Alex said derisively.

Her jaw tightened. "It didn't work out." She folded her hands in her lap.

"Why not?"

"That's not your business."

Alex scowled blackly. "He married you, then dumped you? It doesn't make sense. None of it makes sense."

"He didn't dump me! And it made sense," Daisy insisted. "We hoped it would work. We wanted it to work. Cal's a good man," she said, looking over at the photo on the mantel. She stared at it for a long moment, then turned her gaze and met Alex's, smiling a little sadly. "He's been a good father."

"But not Charlie's only father!" Alex insisted.

"He knows he has a biological father. Well, as much as any four-year-old understands that. He knows he has two fathers. I figured I could explain you more to him as he got older."

"I'll explain myself to him now."

"No," Daisy said. "Not until I know how you feel."

"You know damn well how I feel. I want my son!"

Their gazes locked, dueled. And in the silence of battle, the stairs creaked.

"Mommy?"

Daisy's head jerked up to see Charlie peering over the bannister halfway down them. Alex stared up at him, too. Dear God, had he heard?

Daisy hurried up the stairs and scooped him up into her arms. "What is it, sweetie?"

"My arm hurts," he whimpered, and tucked his head between her jaw and her shoulder. He clung to her, but his gaze was fixed on Alex who was slowly coming to his feet.

Daisy shifted so that her body blocked his view. "I know." She kissed his hair and cuddled him close. "I wish it didn't. I'll take you back upstairs and sing to you. Okay?"

Charlie nodded. "Can Alex come, too?"

"Alex was just leaving." But she turned and carried Charlie down the stairs. "We'll just say goodnight and see him out the front door." She smiled into Alex's suddenly narrowed gaze. "That will be nice, won't it?" she said to her son.

Solemnly Charlie nodded. He looked at Alex.

Alex looked back with an intensity that made Daisy quiver.

Then Charlie lifted his head off her shoulder. "Night, Alex."

Daisy held her breath as, slowly, Alex shrugged into his suit jacket and crossed the room, stopping mere inches from them. He didn't look at her. He had eyes only for Charlie. To Daisy he looked dark, forbidding and positively scary.

But then he lifted a hand to touch Charlie's cheek and his expression softened, a smile touched the corner of his mouth. "Good night, son."

CHAPTER TEN

I⊤ was like waiting for the other shoe to drop.

Daisy half expected to find Alex standing on the stoop when she got up. But a peek out the curtains as soon as she got up proved that no one was there.

He didn't call, either, though she jumped every time the phone rang.

Charlie, pushing his scrambled eggs around his plate, wanted to know what the matter was with her. "You're all jumpy," he remarked when a sound on the sidewalk made her flinch.

"Nothing's the matter." Daisy turned away, busying herself putting the dishes in the dishwasher. "Izzy said she and the boys were coming by."

Izzy's had been the first phone call she'd got this morning.

"How is he?" her friend had demanded even before Daisy had dragged herself out of bed.

"Still asleep," Daisy reported. In fact he was asleep on the other side of her bed. She'd got him back to sleep after Alex had finally left, but he'd awakened and come into her room again at five-thirty. Barely able to pry her eyes open, Daisy had taken the easy way out and let him clamber into bed with her. Fortunately he'd gone straight back to sleep, and when Izzy had rung at eight, he was still dead to the world.

"Sorry. We've been up for hours thinking about him."

"He's going to be fine," Daisy assured her. At least his arm was. How his life was going to change now that Alex was going to be part of it, she didn't know. But at least Alex had been kind last night. He'd actually behaved—toward Charlie—very well. Maybe, given that, he would be fine. And kids were resilient.

It was her own resilience Daisy was worried about.

How was she going to deal with Alexandros Antonides in her life?

She didn't want to think about it. So when Izzy asked if they could come and see Charlie in the afternoon, Daisy said yes without hesitation. The distraction would do them both good.

By midafternoon with no Rip and no Crash, Charlie was getting restless. Daisy had watched a Disney DVD with him, then read him a couple of dozen picture books. She tried unsuccessfully to talk him into a nap.

"I'm too big for naps," he told her. "An' I'm not tired."

No, just cranky. She had a photo shoot to finish editing before tomorrow afternoon. So she brought her laptop down to the living room and worked on it there while Charlie played with his cars and his Legos on the floor.

"Maybe that Alex will come back," he said hopefully, looking up from his cars.

"Mmm." Daisy didn't encourage that line of thinking. A man who had been as adamant as Alex had been about not wanting children might have had a brief change of heart when faced with a little boy who looked very much like his beloved deceased brother.

But having a son was a huge responsibility. And it wasn't one that you could just pick up and put down as the whim struck you. Alex wasn't a fool. He had to realize that. It was possible that Alex had gone home in the early hours of the morning, thought about the implications of having a son, and come to the conclusion that he'd made the right decision five years ago. Whatever he decided, Daisy was determined that she wouldn't let him upset Charlie's life to suit himself.

She didn't have time to think about it more because finally the doorbell rang.

"They're here!" Charlie scrambled up from the floor and raced to open the door.

Daisy unlocked the door, and Charlie tugged it open.

Rip MacCauley took one look at Charlie's cast and said, "Oh, wow. Your cast is blue? That's cool."

The first smile of the day flickered across Charlie's face. "You think?"

"Oh, yeah," Rip said, coming in and taking off his jacket. "I only ever had a white one."

"Mine was purple when I broke my ankle," Crash announced. "Here. This is for you." He thrust a package wrapped in newspaper comics into Charlie's hand.

"A little something to keep him busy," Izzy told Daisy as the boys headed instinctively for the cars and the Legos on the floor and she followed Daisy into the kitchen. "Rip and Crash have been really worried. They seem to think they're indestructible, but when Charlie got hurt, they were, like, 'Oh, no! What if he dies?' They felt very responsible. As well they should, Finn says."

"Finn being such a pattern card of model behavior." Daisy grinned.

Izzy laughed. "That's what I said." She perched

on a bar stool while Daisy made them coffee. "I was amazed when Finn got home so quickly last night. Why didn't you let him stay for a bit and help you with Charlie?"

"No point. We were fine." And she was very glad he hadn't been there to witness the meeting of Alex and his son.

"I'm sorry we interrupted your evening. How was the Plaza? Tell all." Izzy leaned forward eagerly.

It took Daisy a moment to even begin to remember the details, so much had happened in the meantime. "It was…fine," she said vaguely. "The Plaza is elegant, of course. The dinner was wonderful," she added dutifully, because "fine" wasn't going to satisfy Izzy.

"And the dress?"

"It was fantastic."

"Knocked his socks off?" Izzy's eyes were bright.

"It wasn't supposed to knock his socks off," Daisy reminded her. "He's got a girlfriend."

Izzy looked disappointed. But then she shrugged philosophically. "So you had a good time."

Daisy did her best to sound bright and enthusiastic about the evening. She didn't tell Izzy that Alex had turned up at the hospital. She didn't mention anything that happened after that. Until she had some idea of what Alex intended, she wasn't borrowing trouble—or discussing him with anyone.

She was glad Izzy and the boys came because it took the edge off Charlie's boredom and irritability. The matchbox cars that Rip and Crash brought him were a big hit. But Daisy was, honestly, glad when they left again because it was hard to give the impression of cheerful equanimity when she felt edgy and stressed and as if her world was splintering into a million pieces. She left Charlie playing with his cars on the floor in the living room and retreated to the kitchen to wash up the cups and plates from the MacCauleys' visit.

And then the doorbell rang.

"It's Alex!" Charlie yelled, jumping up and running to the door.

Wiping nervous hands on the sides of her jeans, Daisy followed him to answer it. She dragged the door open a few inches and, as always, felt her heart do a somersault in her chest at the mere sight of him.

Gone, of course, was the formal wear of last evening. This afternoon Alex was in jeans and a hunter-green down jacket, his dark hair windblown and dusted with snowflakes, his jaw stubbled. His eyes were bloodshot, but they met hers squarely.

"Daisy." His voice was soft but firm, and gravelly as if he hadn't slept.

"Alex," she replied, holding herself rigid, trying to relax, but unable to. Still she swallowed and tried to sound cordial and polite.

"Hi, Alex." Charlie poked his head around to beam up at the man on the doorstep. "Come 'n' see my new cars."

"Cars?" Alex grinned and stepped across the threshold.

Daisy backed up hastily. "Charlie's much better," she said as he brushed past. "You didn't have to come."

He gave her a look so intense it could have leveled buildings. "I wanted to come." Then he turned his attention to Charlie. "You're better, are you?" he said, his tone far lighter. "Good. I thought maybe we could go to the park."

"The park?" Daisy echoed doubtfully.

But Charlie cheered. Obviously no one had told him he was an invalid.

"But let's see your new cars first." Alex was already shedding his jacket, dropping down onto the floor next to Charlie, making himself at home.

Charlie was clearly delighted to have the attention. He showed Alex the new set of Matchbox cars that Rip and Crash had given him. "Sports cars," he told Alex eagerly. "They go really fast. See?" He raced them around on the floor, making car noises.

Alex stretched out his long legs and leaned back on an elbow, watching, not just indulgently, but with real interest. He picked up the cars by turn, examining them, commenting knowledgeably because, of course, he knew all about cars. It must come standard issue with the Y chromosome.

Daisy stood there, watching, unable to pull herself away. Seeing the two of them together—father and son—was something she'd barely ever dreamed of. Hearing Charlie's eager chatter and Alex's low baritone in reply set something deep inside her quivering, aching.

Wanting. Far too much.

Abruptly she wheeled away. "I'll be upstairs," she said. "I have work to do."

He had come to see Charlie, not her. And while it was hardly an honest introduction to the demands of fatherhood, if he came looking for reinforcements in fifteen minutes, she'd know it wasn't going to last.

Charlie came in half an hour later. "Alex an' me want to go to the park. He says to ask if you want to go along."

Annoyed that he would presume to decide what

he and Charlie were going to do without consulting her, Daisy hurried downstairs.

The Legos and Matchbox cars had been neatly put away and Alex was zipping up his jacket. "Good," he said. "You're coming, too."

"You don't presume. You should have asked!"

"Charlie did ask."

Charlie bobbed his head. "I said we wanted to go, and did you want to come."

Daisy opened her mouth, then closed it again. "Fine," she said shortly. "I'll come."

It was torture, seeing him with Charlie, being with him herself, acting as though they were some lovely happy family, all the while knowing it was a sham.

"Take it easy," Alex said in an undertone as she jerkily shoved her arms into her jacket. "I'm not going to steal my son."

My son, she wanted to correct him. *And no, you're damned well not!*

But Alex had turned and was helping Charlie with his jacket. Daisy wanted to push him away and do it herself. But one look told her that Charlie was more patient with Alex helping than he would have been with her. And Alex did take the time to show him how to do it himself—except for the zipping up part.

"Guess we'll have to help with that," he said easily, then zipped the jacket up to Charlie's chin. Then rising again, he reached down to ruffle the little boy's hair.

It was a casual movement, but it already spoke of a connection that made Daisy's insides clench, especially when Charlie flashed him a happy grin.

Turning abruptly, she called Murphy and snapped on his leash. Then the four of them went out the door and headed to the park—just like a family.

She shouldn't have come. She should have stayed back in her office and got more work done. But the temptation of watching Alex with Charlie was too great. It was terrifying, too. But Charlie was having such a good time.

There was still lots of snow on the ground. Once they got to the park, they built a snowman. And they had a snowball fight. Then Charlie made snow angels.

"A snow devil more like," Daisy said, laughing as she watched him, then taking photos with the small pocket-size camera she always carried. She got quite a few of Charlie and Alex rolling balls to make the snowman, then more of Alex lifting Charlie onto his shoulders so he could put an old hat on the snowman's head.

They were laughing as they did it, Alex lurching

around in the snow while Charlie gripped Alex's hair with his free hand and laughed madly. Then Alex tipped his head back to grin up at his son, and the look they shared made Daisy feel as if she'd caught a snowball square in the heart.

Later she nearly did as she helped Charlie pelt Alex with snowballs. She got several shots of Charlie and Alex throwing them at each other. Then Alex took the camera out of her hand.

"What are you doing?" She tried to grab it back.

But Alex held it out of her reach, his green eyes mischievous. "Go play with your son."

Self-consciously at first, Daisy did. But then she got caught up in Charlie's enthusiasm. And while she pushed Charlie on a swing and helped him build a little snow dog to go with the snowman, Alex took pictures. Finally, when Daisy said it was time to leave, he set the camera's timer and hauled them all into a picture together, scooping Charlie up into one arm while he flung the other around Daisy.

And once more when his arm pulled her close, Daisy felt the hum of electricity between them. She felt desire all over again, and knew it for the hopeless feeling it was. It was a relief when the timer went off, the shutter clicked, and he let her go, slung Charlie onto his shoulders and they all walked home.

On the doorstep, when Alex set him down, Daisy smiled politely. "Thank you. He enjoyed that."

"Did you?" Alex asked.

She heard the pointedness of his tone and chose to ignore it. "Of course." She fumbled to get the key in the lock. He was wearing sunglasses and before she'd turned away she couldn't read his expression, but she could still feel the intensity of his gaze.

"Good." He took the key out of her hand and opened the door himself. Then he pushed it open, let them go in, then followed and shut it behind him.

"I need to get dinner started. Don't let us keep you. I'm sure you have things to do." Daisy said briskly and, slipping off her jacket, started toward the kitchen.

"We can get takeout. What do you like?"

"I'm making stew. Charlie likes it."

"So do I." Alex smiled guilelessly.

"Alex can stay, can't he?" Charlie asked.

What was a mother to do? Of course she had to be polite. She was teaching Charlie to be polite.

The evening was interminable. Dinner. Then Charlie's bath. Then bedtime stories. And awareness of Alex at every single moment. Watching him with Charlie, catching him looking at her when he thought she wasn't noticing. Charlie's stories took forever, even though Alex read several of them. Prayers were longer, too, because Alex, of course, was added to them.

"No singing tonight," Daisy decreed before Charlie could even suggest it. "You need to go to sleep. Remember, your class is going to the zoo tomorrow." The preschool trip to the Bronx Zoo—and a program about animals in winter—had been much anticipated.

Now Charlie looked up from his pillow and asked, "Can Alex come?"

"No," Daisy said without giving Alex a chance to reply.

"But—"

"I have to work," Alex said, sounding regretful. "But we had fun today. We'll do this again."

Charlie popped up. "When?"

"That depends on how well and how fast you go to sleep now," Daisy said, no stranger to manipulative children. She gave him a speaking look.

Charlie sighed, sank back against the pillow and shut his eyes. "I'm sleepin'."

"So I see," Daisy said drily, bending to kiss him. "Good night, Mr. Sleepyhead."

"Night," Charlie murmured, not opening his eyes.

She stepped back, and found that Alex had taken her place at Charlie's bedside. He brushed a hand over Charlie's head, then dropped to one knee and pressed a light kiss on Charlie's forehead.

The boy's eyes popped open and small hard arms and one very hard blue cast wrapped themselves around Alex's neck.

Alex stiffened. And Daisy held her breath.

Then slowly his posture eased, and his arms went around Charlie, too. He scooped the boy up for a fierce hug, burying his face in the crook of Charlie's neck. Then slowly he drew back and lowered the boy to the pillows again. "G'night, sport." His voice was rough. He straightened and stood looking down at the little boy for a long moment.

Then his gaze turned to Daisy. Their eyes met. She shut off the light and headed down to the kitchen.

If he wanted to talk, he could do it while she washed the dinner dishes. But frankly, she didn't know what else there was to say. She began to run water in the sink, all the while aware of exactly where he was, hip propped against the counter beside the refrigerator, watching her.

"Sorry I didn't get here earlier," he said over the running water.

"You didn't need to come at all." Daisy set the plates in the soapy water.

"Of course I needed to come. But I had to get hold of Caroline. I needed to tell her first."

Daisy did turn then. "That you had a son? How did she take that after your 'no children ever' edict?"

Alex's mouth twisted wryly. "She was…surprised."

"I'll bet." Daisy turned away again, picking up a mug and scrubbing it so furiously that the tiny sprays of yellow primroses on it threatened to disappear.

"But she understands."

Daisy's teeth came together as she swallowed half a dozen remarks that were far snarkier than the previous one. "I don't want her *understanding*. If she's like you, she doesn't want kids around!"

"She won't have them. We've broken it off."

Daisy stared at him. "What?"

Alex lifted his shoulders. "Circumstances changed. I called Amalie, too. Told her I was cancelling the rest of our agreement. My matchmaker," Alex said when Daisy stared at him blankly.

She was still processing Caroline's departure. "Why?"

"Because I don't need one now. Obviously. She gets her money anyway, so she doesn't care. She wished me all the best." He paused, then exhaled slowly and said, "So, the decks are clear."

There was a moment's stark silence as the implication of his words set in. Daisy felt a sudden chill but it started inside her, not out.

"Clear," she echoed. "Clear for what?"

But as soon as she asked, she knew she couldn't let him answer. She already knew—and she didn't want to hear it. "For you to be noble? For you to do something stupid like ask me to marry you?"

Alex stared at her, taken aback. "Damned right I want to marry you. Why the hell not? It makes perfect sense."

Exactly what she wanted to hear. Daisy wasn't cold any longer, she was burning up. She wouldn't have been surprised if steam was coming out of her ears.

"You're just like Cal! What is it with men, anyway? Why do you always think you can make the world act the way you want it to?"

"Daisy—"

"It's all control with you, isn't it?"

"Daisy, stop it! Stop being stupid. And this has

nothing to do with your ex or anyone else." He shoved away from where he was leaning against the countertop and came toward her. "Be sensible, Daisy. I want to—"

"No. Don't do it, Alex," she said fiercely. "Don't say it. I don't want to hear it." She flung the sponge away and put her hands over her ears. "I won't!"

Of all the bloody-minded females!

Alex couldn't believe it! But Daisy was glaring at him, her cheeks flushed, her eyes flashing. She'd flung the sponge into the sink and put her hands over her ears, defying him to...what?

Propose?

Of course he was damned well going to propose. It was the right thing to do. If he had fathered a child—and he quite obviously had—it was his duty to marry his child's mother, be her husband, a father to their child and...and then what?

Live happily ever after?

He wouldn't let himself think about that.

Because in his experience, people didn't get to. Well, maybe some did. But how did you know? How could you ever be sure?

You couldn't. But the decision was no longer his. He'd made it five years ago when he'd made love to Daisy. He'd spent all night coming to terms with what that meant, and he was ready to do it. Determined to do it.

And now...

Now he didn't have to.

Just like that, Daisy had popped his balloon of self-righteous nobility before he'd even had a chance to let it fly.

He should be relieved, Alex told himself. Somewhere deep down, he supposed he *was* relieved. But at the same time, he was madder than hell. He didn't like being dismissed, being told his presence wasn't needed, wasn't valued.

And if she expected he would just turn around and walk away, she was bloody well out of her mind. At least she'd taken her hands off her ears now and had turned back to the pots and pans with which she was making an almighty racket.

Alex scowled at her back. "I seem to recall," he pointed out, "that you wanted marriage."

The pots continued to clatter. She shot him a quick furious glance over her shoulder. "Five years ago, yes. When I was besotted, yes. When I thought you loved me, too. Not now! I don't want you now!"

It surprised him that her words actually hurt. They made him stiffen as if he could defend himself against them, against her. His jaw felt as tight as a steel trap. "Fine," he said tersely. "You don't have to 'have' me."

Daisy turned, a look of consternation flicked across her features, followed by a faint sheepish smile of relief. "Well, um, good. Thank you," she said gruffly.

"But that doesn't mean you're getting rid of me."

She blinked. "But—"

"For God's sake, Daisy. You have my son! You might not have seen fit to tell me, but I know it now. And I'm not going to walk out of his life. I want to be part of it. I want him to be part of mine."

"For how long? Are you going to be buddies like you were today? For as long as it suits you? Are you going to be here when he needs you or are you going to walk when the going gets tough? Do you imagine you can be here and not *care,* Alex? You said—you told me plainly—brutally—that you didn't want to care—about anyone!" Her eyes flashed with accusation.

"You never let me care," he pointed out, trying to sound calmer than he felt. "You didn't even tell me he existed!"

"To protect him! To protect him from the knowledge that for you love is a one-way street!"

Stung, for a moment Alex didn't reply. Deliberately he swallowed his discomfort at the truth of her words. But at the same time, he lashed back. "Is that what it is?" he challenged her. "Or maybe—" he flung at her because, damn it, he wasn't the only one in the wrong "—it's all about protecting yourself!"

"I don't need to protect myself from you anymore. I know the score now. But Charlie doesn't. He'll give his love, wholly and completely, to you! To a man who can't let himself care—to a man who thinks love is worth nothing! And how do you think that's going to make him feel? I know what that's like, remember? And I wasn't four! I know what's right for my son!"

"And you're the arbiter of all things 'right' in Charlie's life?"

"I know him better than anyone. I love him more than anyone. I want the best for him."

"The best thing would be if he had a family," Alex told her flatly. "And you know it."

Daisy didn't reply. She just stared at him stonily. Then she reached for a towel, dried her hands on it, and marched past him, heading straight into the living room where she twisted the locks and yanked open the door. "I think it's time you left now."

Alex followed her into the living room, but he

stopped there, staring at her, trying to fathom what was going on in her head. She wasn't being sensible, wasn't being rational.

"You know I'm right, Daisy."

She just looked at him, then at the door. When he still didn't move, she yanked his jacket off the hook where he'd hung it and thrust it at him. "Goodbye, Alex."

Wordlessly he reached out and took it, shrugged it on and zipped it up. "Fine. I'll go. But this isn't over. I'll be back. And while I'm gone, don't just think about Charlie. Think about what you want, too."

And he pulled her into his arms and took her mouth with his.

He'd been wanting to do this all day, all yesterday, every minute, it seemed, since he'd kissed her last. The hunger was so fierce he ached with it.

Now he felt her whole body stiffen. She raised her arms between them, her forearms pressing against his chest as if to hold him off. It didn't matter. While he would have liked to feel her body melt against him, to have her arms wrap around him, to know her eagerness matched his, he didn't need it to prove his point.

He had his lips to convince her, to taste her, to tease her. He had his tongue to touch her lips, to part them, to slip between and find her sweetness. God, she made him crazy, made his whole being quiver with need, made the blood sing in his veins.

He wasn't going to let her pretend that it meant nothing. Kissing Daisy *never* meant nothing. Kissing Daisy was amazing, wild, always potent, always drugging. Kissing Daisy always made his heart slam against the wall of his chest, made his loins tighten and his body hum with desire.

And damn it, he knew—absolutely knew—it was the same for her.

She fought it. He could feel her resisting. But she was fighting herself, not him. Her lips trembled, pressed together, denied him. But she denied herself, as well.

So he touched them anyway. He drew a line with his tongue, coaxed, teased. And they gave, opened just a fraction. He took advantage, darted within. He heard her whimper, and her fingers opened to clutch his jacket, hanging on. Her lips softened, parted farther. And he felt a jolt as her tongue tangled with his.

Yes, like that. It was always like that between them. Always had been. Alex wanted to cheer, to exult, to press his advantage and take them where they both wanted to go. He wanted to slide his fingers beneath her sweater and stroke her curves, her breasts, her very bones. He wanted to tease beneath the waistband of her jeans, slide his fingers south, touch her—there. Damn she was killing him. His breath came hard and fast. He wanted to taste, to tease, to sample and suckle. He wanted to devour. He wrapped her in his arms, thrust his fingers in her hair, kissed her hard one more time.

Then he pulled back, dragging in lungfuls of air as he looked down into her stunned feverish gaze. "While you're thinking," he said roughly, "think about that."

Her palm connected with his cheek so fast he didn't even see it coming.

"What the hell was that for?" he demanded. His fingers curled. He jammed his hands in his pockets.

"What was the kiss for?" she countered furiously.

His gaze narrowed. "*That's* why you slapped me? For reminding you that we had something good?"

"I don't need any reminders, thank you very much. And it turns out we didn't have anything at all."

"You don't believe that."

"I do. And I don't need you trying to bribe me with sex."

He gaped at her. "Bribe you?"

Her eyes flashed. "Bribe me, get around me, coerce me, make me do what you want because I'm somehow susceptible to you! Call it what you like. It's not going to work."

"For God's sake, Daisy." He raked fingers through his hair. "I was trying to show you it isn't all about Charlie."

"No, it isn't. It's all about you—what you want, when you want it, and not when you don't. You don't love Charlie. You don't love anyone. You don't want to. You push people away. At least Cal wanted to," she spat at him furiously.

"Cal?" he retorted. "This is all about Cal? All about your 'failed' marriage? Has it really made you that bitter?"

"I'm not bitter at all. Not at Cal. Not at our marriage." She lifted her chin as if defying him to argue. "We went into it with our eyes open."

He watched her, saw a host of conflicting expressions cross her face. Then she lifted a shoulder as if shrugging off a burden and said, "Cal is gay."

Alex stared at her.

"He's my friend. And he didn't have a lover. So when he saw what I was going through, he tried to make it easier for me." She ran her tongue over her lips. "He was convinced that he could will himself to love whoever he wanted to love." She shrugged. "He believes in the same things I do—commitment, long-term relationships, responsibility. Love."

Alex's gaze narrowed.

"He never lied to me. And I didn't lie to him. He knew I loved you. He knew you didn't love me. He offered his name, his support, everything he could. And I did the same for him. But—" she lifted her shoulders "—it wasn't enough. We tried to make it work. It didn't. In the end we knew that. We'll always be friends. But there's more to real love, real marriage than that. And we both wanted…more."

"I'm offering you more," Alex pointed out indignantly.

Daisy just looked at him. She took a slow breath, then swallowed and shook her head. "No, Alex. You're not. You're offering far, far less."

She pushed him out the door and closed it after him.

CHAPTER ELEVEN

DAISY leaned against the door, tears blurring her eyes. She dashed them away with a shaking hand. Of course he thought she was mad. The way he'd looked at her, patent disbelief in his eyes.

He was offering her marriage, wasn't he? Hadn't that been her heart's desire five years ago?

Yes, then. Not now.

Because this was exactly the sort of "marriage" he would have been offering Caroline. A wedding, a legal, convenient version of friends with benefits. Now as she stood with her back to the front door, still hearing Alex's footfalls moving quickly away, Daisy wiped a hand over her face, touched the tears, wanted to deny them. Knew she couldn't.

They were as real as the truth she'd just told Alex: marriages of convenience didn't work. Not for her. She and Cal had done their best. But friendship and responsibility only went so far.

They were only a part of the deep abiding fullness of heart, soul, mind and body that real love was.

She knew it wasn't easy. She knew, just as Alex knew, that real love hurt.

She didn't care. If she could have the love, she could endure the pain. She'd been raised in the real love of her parents' marriage. She remembered their joys and their sorrows. She remembered all too well her mother's pain at her father's death.

But she remembered, too, the sight of her mother smiling through her tears as she'd said, "I don't regret it for an instant. Loving Jack was worth all of this."

This was sometimes heartache, sometimes pain, sometimes joy, sometimes the simple act of heart-deep sharing.

Daisy wanted that.

She had the pain part down pat, she thought, tears streaming down her face.

But she knew she'd done the right thing—even if Alex had been right, that she'd been protecting herself. If marrying Cal had been a mistake, marrying Alex would be a disaster—because she could not stop loving him, and he didn't know what real love was.

He couldn't draw a straight line.

He broke the lead in all his mechanical pencils. He snapped the nib off his best drawing pen. His hands shook so badly as he sat at his desk and tried to find the calm he always felt designing, that he crumpled up page after page of the paper in his sketchbook.

Finally Alex threw the whole damn thing out and went to stand and stare out the window, dragging in deep breaths. But for once even the sight of the spectacular Manhattan skyline didn't soothe his furious soul.

He pressed his forehead against the cold glass of the window, then lifted a hand and rubbed it against his stubbled cheek.

The physical sting of Daisy's palm was long gone. But the emotional sting was imprinted on his soul. So were the words she'd flung at him: *It's all about you. You don't love Charlie. You don't love anyone. You don't want to.*

His throat tightened. His eyes blurred. He sucked in another breath and shook his head, wanting to deny it.

But he couldn't. Not entirely. At least a part of what she said was true: He *hadn't* wanted to.

For years—ever since Vass's death and his parents' divorce—Alex had done his best to make sure that anything as messy and painful as love would not be a part of his world. He'd deliberately built himself a life without it. He had his business, his design projects, his friends, and recently he'd figured that he could do marriage as long as it was on his terms, where his wife didn't want anything deeper or more demanding than he did.

He'd wanted a world he could control.

Which was why he had turned his back on Daisy five years ago.

She had threatened his control. She had bowled him over that weekend, had loved and given and enchanted in equal measures. He'd never met anyone so unguarded, so genuine, so warm and real.

Letting Daisy into his life would have been opening himself up to a tidal wave of emotions he couldn't control, a future he couldn't predict, the possibility for pain he didn't ever want to experience again.

God knew what would happened if he let down his guard.

So he hadn't. He'd turned away from her warmth, rejected her love, shut her out of his life. And having done so, he'd thought he was safe.

He was wrong.

But she was wrong, too.

Daisy had thought he *couldn't* love, and Alex had believed he *wouldn't*.

But God help him, he did. He loved Charlie. He'd only had to see the boy, watch the joy of life in his eyes, listen to him, hold his hand, touch his hair—and he loved. But more than that, before he recognized that he loved Charlie, he knew he loved her.

Daisy.

In spite of himself and his determined intentions, the day Daisy had come into his life, she had created a tiny rent in his armor. She had pierced his defenses, had touched his heart and planted a seed deep in his soul. For two days she had given him a glimpse of what life could be like if he had dared to let it grow.

He hadn't. He'd turned his back. But while he thought he'd walked away heart-whole, it wasn't true.

The minute he'd seen her again this autumn, everything he had felt when he'd been with her the first time—the need, the emotion, the connection—the sense that the world was a brighter, warmer, fuller, more welcoming place—had broken through.

He hadn't given in, of course. Though he had felt the attraction all over again, he'd still tried to do it his way—to control it. To control her.

He couldn't.

She wouldn't let him.

He knew what she wanted. Demanded. A real future, a no-holds-barred willingness to love and, admitting that love, to face the possibility of pain, of loss of control, of helplessness—all the things he'd said no to.

He didn't know if he could do it now.

But he loved. He had no choice. It was simply there—in him. For better or worse. But he knew he couldn't face the future until he was able to face the past.

Rubbing a hand over his face, Alex turned away from the window, from the cool remote perfection of the distant skyline, to the emotional minefield that he carried inside him. He padded into his bedroom.

The room was spare, unadorned. It held a wide bed, a tall oak chest of drawers, a closet. Nothing more. He went to the chest of drawers, then crouched down and pulled open the bottom drawer.

It was empty except for one thing—a single sturdy, flat, dark green cardboard box, perhaps a foot-square, two inches deep.

For a long minute, he just looked at it. Didn't immediately reach for it. Didn't really want to touch it even yet.

He hadn't touched it except when he'd moved it, since he'd left for university at the age of eighteen. He hadn't opened it since he'd put the lid on it when his parents separated, when they sold the house, when his mother moved to Athens and his father to Corfu.

"Don't look back," his father had said as he'd sold off everything and buried himself in his scholarly books.

But Alex had put the things that mattered in that box, the things he couldn't let go of, even if he couldn't bring himself to look at them.

He'd carried the box with him ever since. He'd taken it to university in London, to his first job in Brussels, to the dozen or so places he'd lived in his adult life. He had brought it with him here.

Wherever he was, he always put it carefully in its own drawer where he wouldn't accidentally stumble across it when he was looking for something else. He didn't want to be blindsided when he wasn't prepared.

Someday, he always promised himself, he would open it. When the time was right he would once again let himself remember. But as time had passed, he'd learned to cope, he'd shut off the past, had refused to give it the power to hurt him. It was easier to forget. The time had never been right.

Until now.

Now he hurt anyway. Now Daisy's words had cut right through his protective shield, had looked inside him and found him wanting.

His hands shook as he drew the box out of the drawer and carried it over to sit on the bed with it. He was surprised how light it was. In his imagination it was the heaviest thing he owned.

He ran his fingers over the top, then carefully eased the lid off and set it aside. There were only a handful of things within—and just as he had feared, the sight of them brought a thousand memories flooding back.

There was the postcard of the Matterhorn that Vass had sent him when he was six and Vass was nine. Vass had been with their father in Switzerland. "It's s'cool," he had written. "You and me will climb it someday."

They hadn't, of course. But when Vass came home, they'd begun climbing the cliffs by their island home with eager purpose. Just as they'd earnestly practiced tying ship's knots in the two feet of line that lay in the box, as well.

"Learn to tie the knots and I'll teach you to sail," their father had said.

Now Alex drew the piece of line out of the box and his fingers moved automatically to make a Spanish bowline, a clove hitch, a figure eight while in his mind's eye he saw the summer days they'd spent on the water, the three of them. He remembered the heat and the sun and the wind—and the stories and the laughter that came with them.

He picked a small reddish-brown pottery shard out next, rubbing his thumb over its worn contours and remembering Vass finding it and saying he was going to grow up and be an archaeologist like Indiana Jones. And there were two very well-used Star Wars figures—Luke and Han, of course— they'd played with for years. There was a painstaking drawing of the Battlestar Galactica that Vass had drawn while he was in the hospital, and a far more precise elegant one that Alex had drawn at the same time because, after all, he was the one who was going to be the architect, not Vass.

And then there was a single silver Porsche Matchbox car.

Alex had faced all the other bits of memorabilia with a tight jaw, a strained smile, blinking eyes.

But the silver Porsche felt like a dagger to his heart.

They had fought over the silver Porsche, he and Vass. It had been his brother's, but Vass had been indifferent until Alex wanted it. And they had fought—actually came to blows—and Vass had punched him in the stomach and he had given Vass a bloody nose.

He stared at the small car now, picked it up and

ran his hands over the lines of its frame. Then he closed his fingers around it until he felt the cold metal bite into his hand. He wanted to feel it. Needed the pain.

It hadn't been Vass's first bloody nose. He'd had several that summer. But this one they hadn't been able to stop. Not until they'd taken him to the doctor. And then there had been murmurs of concern. His mother's worry. His father's pacing. More doctor visits. A flight to Athens to see a specialist. A hospital. Tests.

A diagnosis. Leukemia.

Because of a bloody nose. A bloody nose that was Alex's fault.

It wasn't, of course. He knew that now. But at the time, he was not yet nine years old. He hadn't known—and no one had bothered to reassure him. They'd all been far too worried about Vass. He had been worried, too.

But he'd swallowed his worry and his guilt because there hadn't been time for it, there hadn't been room for it. His parents hadn't even seen it.

When Vass had come home from the hospital the first time, Alex had been scared to go into his room, afraid he might do more damage.

But Vass had said scornfully, "You can't give somebody leukemia. You're not that powerful, brat." Then he'd grinned, Vass's old wonderful "I can do anything" grin, and Alex had had his brother back.

Then he'd believed Vass would recover. Then he'd hoped for the best. Two and a half years later, there was no best.

The last time he'd been in Vass's hospital room, Vass had said, "Keep the Porsche. It's yours."

"I don't want it," Alex had protested, tears streaming down his face.

Now slowly, painfully, he unbent his fingers, and stared at the little car. He rubbed his fingers over it, remembering Vass doing the same thing. He squeezed his eyes shut and saw Vass's frail body and thin pale face, and he let the pain wash over him.

But other memories came, too. Along with the pain, he remembered the good times, the joy, the sharing and laughter. And he knew you couldn't have one without the other.

For years he'd put the Porsche and the memories in a box and tucked them away, unable to face them.

You don't love anyone. You don't want to. Daisy's words echoed in his mind. He heard them again, along with her parting shot: *You're offering far, far less.*

Alex knew what he had to do.

He just hoped to God he could do it.

"'S Christmas!" Charlie jiggled Daisy's shoulder, waking her, peering wide-eyed into her sleep-gritted ones. "An' Santa came!"

The pure joy of youth and belief beamed at her. She rolled over and shoved herself to a sitting position, then reached out to pull him into a fierce hug. "Of course he did. Were you worried?"

Charlie gave her a quick, hard, fierce hug in return, then wriggled out of her grasp, his head shaking to and fro. "Nah. I knew he'd come." He held out a hand to her and Daisy let him pull her to her feet.

"I did, too," she confided, snagging her bathrobe as he dragged her toward the living room, toward the Christmas tree which was already lit with small bright multicolored lights, because obviously Charlie had been there first, poking around.

But he hadn't opened any gifts. He had waited for her. Now he looked at her expectantly.

And deliberately, mustering all the joy she could manage, Daisy put her game face on. "Let me put the coffee on. Then we'll see what Santa brought."

There was no time to brood on Christmas morning. There were gifts to unwrap and ooh-and-aah over. Santa made a just-turned-five-year-old boy very happy. There was a set of Legos and some action figures, three new books, a soccer ball, and a floor mat with the outline of streets and buildings—a city to drive his cars around in. Daisy's mother had sent him a build-it-yourself racetrack for his little cars and a stash of art supplies for rainy days.

Charlie was thrilled. He wanted to play with all of it now. Daisy wanted to let him. But Cal was coming to get Charlie at noon. His parents were already here from Cooperstown and were looking forward to spending the day with Cal and their grandson. All of Cal's siblings and their families were coming, too.

"They'd be happy to see you, too," Cal had assured Daisy last week when they'd discussed plans. "You don't have to be alone."

But Daisy had shaken her head. "I'll be all right. I've booked a photo shoot." She had done it deliberately, agreeing to a plea from one of her old college classmates that she do a four-generation family shoot on Christmas afternoon.

"They're all only here for the day," Josie had apologized when she'd asked. "I know it's probably impossible being Christmas and all…but just in case…"

"Sounds great," Daisy had said firmly. It would keep her from sitting at home alone and miserable. "It'll be fun." She'd pasted a bright determined smile on her face. "If it's nice and there's snow on the ground, we can shoot it in the park."

It was nice. There was even, amazingly enough, a few inches of new snow on the ground. And more was drifting down by the time Cal appeared at the door.

He was smiling and looked happier than she could remember. She knew he'd met someone. It was early days yet, he'd told her last week. But there was a light in his eyes she hadn't ever seen before.

He took one look at her pale face and the dark circles under her own eyes and said, "You look awful."

Daisy laughed wryly. "Thank you very much."

But Cal frowned. "I shouldn't be taking him away from you today. Come with us."

Adamantly Daisy shook her head. "I'm meeting Josie's family at their place at one to do some indoor shots, then we're going to shoot at the Bow Bridge in the park if it's still snowing."

"Come after you finish."

"I'll be fine," she insisted. "Go on. Have a good time." She gave Charlie a hug and a kiss. "Behave."

"I always behave," he said stoutly. "I'm bringin' my new guys to show Grandpa."

"He'll like that." Daisy gave him one more squeeze, then stood up. Her smile was strained. Of course Charlie didn't notice. She hoped Cal didn't, either. "See you tomorrow," she said with all the cheer she could manage. Then she shut the door behind them, leaned back against it, and pressed her hands to her eyes.

It was letting Charlie go, she told herself. This was, after all, the first Christmas that she hadn't had him with her all the time. Always before, after their divorce, Cal had come here and they'd celebrated together. But they both knew that couldn't last. He had a life now—and she had to get one.

Now she scrubbed at her eyes and took a deep, hopefully steadying breath, then she went upstairs to get ready to go, picking out the lenses and filters she wanted to take, determined to keep her mind busy so she wouldn't think about where Charlie was and what he was doing and…

…about Alex.

She *had* to stop thinking about Alex.

It had been two weeks since they'd had their confrontation. Two weeks since she'd spurned his offer of marriage before he could even make it, since she'd told him exactly what she thought of it—and of him—and had shoved him out of the door and out of her life.

He hadn't been back.

Was she surprised? Of course not. It was for the best, really, and she knew it.

What surprised her was how much she cared.

She didn't want to care! She didn't want to miss him, didn't want to remember him sitting on the floor playing with Charlie, didn't want to think about him telling their son a story, didn't want to close her eyes and be plagued by images of him with Charlie in his arms or on his shoulders, the two of them grinning at each other.

She didn't want to remember how proud she'd felt the night he'd got the award for his hospital design, how intently she'd listened when he'd told her about his inspiration for it, how much she heard and understood what he didn't ever say.

She didn't want to think about him—and she couldn't seem to stop.

Now she finished packing her gear bag, slipped on her puffy, bright blue down jacket and headed toward the park.

It was Christmas. A time of hope. A time to put the past behind her and move on. She squared her shoulders, and picked up her bag. Maybe after she'd finished Josie's family's photo shoot, she would go ice skating, meet the man of her dreams, fall in love.

Fairy tales. Would she never learn?

Daisy sighed and headed for Josie's place.

Four generations of the Costello family were ready and waiting. Josie swept Daisy into their Fifth Avenue sixth floor apartment overlooking the park, equal measures eager and apologetic. They were so glad to have her take photos of their family holiday, they were so sorry they were taking her away from her own family today of all days.

"It's all right," Daisy assured them. "I'm glad to do it."

It was every bit the distraction she had hoped. The seven children—cousins who didn't see each other often—along with their parents, grandparents and two great-grandparents, were a noisy energetic mob. And Daisy, intrigued by the possibilities, threw herself into the work.

She did a series of family groups, then gathered them around the table, shot Josie's grandfather slicing the turkey, her grandmother helping the youngest grandson fill his plate. She caught two cousins playing chess in front of the fire, three little girl cousins playing dress-up with the small trunk of fancy clothes one had got for Christmas.

It was the perfect family Christmas, the kind she'd seen in movies and on TV. The kind she'd always wanted for herself. And especially for Charlie.

She shot their preening and their giggling. She shot four generations of Costello men watching football on television, simultaneously cheering or groaning. She had all the children make a human pyramid that mimicked the Christmas tree.

Then, as soon as she shot that, she said, "Let's go to the park," before things got rowdy, which the human pyramid showed signs of becoming.

The snow was still falling, picture-perfect, when they got to the Bow Bridge. She posed them there and did a couple of formal shots for posterity while passersby, walking off their Christmas dinners, stopped and watched then, smiling, moved on.

Daisy didn't pay them any mind. She glanced their way, then turned back to shoot a series of photos of great-grandpa and grandpa and two little grandsons building a snowman. The girls were making snow angels, their colorful scarves flung out against the snow as they moved their arms and legs. They danced and played and she captured it all—the grace, the laughter—mothers and daughters, grandmothers, great-grandmother and granddaughters. The boys were wrestling in the snow now, pelting each other with snowballs, laughing madly.

Family.

How she envied them their family. She tried to shove the thought away even as it tightened her throat, made her swallow hard. She blinked hard and stopped shooting for a moment, needing to turn away.

Several people who had been watching, smiled at her and scuffed their feet and moved away. She got a grip, started to turn back, then caught a glimpse of someone else out of the corner of her eye.

Her gaze stopped, jerked back, dismissed it. She turned to shoot the snowball-throwing boys again. But her heart was beating faster as she edged around to get a different angle, to look west without turning her head.

He was still there, standing in the shadows beneath the trees.

Lean, tall. Dark wind-blown hair. Wearing jeans and a hunter-green down jacket.

"Lookit me!" one of the Costello boys shouted. He had scrambled up into the crook of a tree and peered down at her.

Daisy turned, focused, shot. Then she swivelled again, taking more shots of the snowball fight, but not even looking at what she was shooting.

She was trying to squint past the camera, to get a better look. He was too far away to be sure. But the last time she'd seen Alex he'd worn a jacket like that.

Surely it wasn't. It couldn't be. It was her stupid fairy-tale-obsessed mind playing tricks on her.

She turned and aimed her shots at the snowman builders now. Grandpa had the littlest boy on his shoulders to loop a scarf around the snowman's neck. Daisy shot it all. That was what she was here for.

When she turned around again, she expected the man to be gone. He was leaning against the tree, hands in his pockets, staring steadily at her.

Daisy raised her camera and pointed it. She zoomed in, and caught her breath.

Slowly Alex nodded at her.

But he didn't move, didn't come closer. Just leaned against the tree, as if he was waiting for a bus or something!

"Are your fingers freezing? Daisy? Daisy?"

She turned, realizing that Josie had been talking to her. "N-no. I'm fine. I— Fine." She glanced back.

He was still there.

"I think we'll call it quits if you've got enough," Josie said. "The little ones and great-grandma are getting cold. I am, too," she admitted, blowing on her hands. "But it's been such fun. Will you come with us? We're going to make cocoa for the kids and hot toddies for the grown-ups."

The panicky desperate part of Daisy wanted to jump at the invitation. Whatever Alex was doing there, he was there on purpose. He had something to say. And Daisy was sure she didn't want to hear it.

But if she didn't hear it now, he'd find another time. And at least she wouldn't have to worry about Charlie overhearing.

"Thanks," she said to Josie. "But I'll just go on home. I loved doing it, though. I'll have the proofs for you by the end of the week."

"Fantastic." Josie gave her a hug. "You were brilliant. And we had a blast. We'll remember it always."

Daisy smiled wanly. She had a feeling she would, too.

With cheery goodbyes and fierce hugs from several small children and a couple of great-grandparents, Daisy began to pack up her gear while the Costellos headed back across the park.

She focused securing the lenses in her camera bag. She didn't look around, ignored the sound of footsteps through the snow. But her heart was going like a jackhammer in her chest. She straightened just as a shadow fell across her.

"Daisy." His voice was soft and gruff, surprisingly hesitant.

Steeling herself, she turned. The sight that met her eyes was a surprise, too. This wasn't the smooth confident man she expected to see. This Alex's jaw was stubbled with at least a day's worth of beard. This Alex's eyes were bloodshot and shadowed. As she stared, his jaw bunched and tightened. He ran the tip of his tongue between his lips, then pressed them together again.

"Alex." She nodded carefully, determinedly giving nothing away, particularly encouragement. The last thing she needed was to fight this battle again.

For a long moment he didn't speak, either, and Daisy wondered if she ought to just step around him, head home. Maybe he'd just been walking in the park, had happened on her by accident. God knew perverse things like that could happen.

"You were right," he said abruptly. "What you said."

Daisy blinked. What she'd said? What had she said? Uncertainly she shook her head.

"That I didn't want to love. That I pushed people away." He answered the question before she even had to ask. He said the words quickly, as if he needed to get past them. Then he said again more slowly, "I didn't want to. Then." Pale green eyes met hers.

Then? Which meant…what? Daisy felt herself tense, but didn't move. She searched his gaze, tried to hear the words he never said.

Then he took a breath and said them. "I loved my brother," he said, the words coming out on a harsh breath. "And I thought I killed him."

"What?" She stared at him, aghast.

He shook his head. "We had a fight…over a car. A toy. I was *eight*," he said harshly. "And I gave him a bloody nose. He bled and bled. They said he had leukemia. I thought…" He shook his head, anguished. "I wasn't even nine," he said. "I didn't know."

"Oh, Alex." She just looked at him. She'd known about his brother. She hadn't known this.

"He said I didn't. But he just kept getting sicker. And…then he died." Now she could hear him dragging the words out. "My parents were shell-shocked. Destroyed. They couldn't help each other. They couldn't even look at me."

"It wasn't your fault!"

"I know that now. But we don't talk much in my family, not about…" He swallowed, then looked past her over her shoulder, staring into the distance, his eyes bright with unshed tears. Whatever he was seeing, Daisy was sure it wasn't in Central Park.

He brought his gaze back to hers, his eyes filled with pain. "When I was ten years old I thought I'd killed my brother and ended our family." His throat worked. "I loved all of them."

And she had told him he didn't love anyone.

"I'm sorry." Her words came out as brokenly as his. She wanted to reach out, to touch his sleeve, to put her arms around him. She had no right. "I'm so sorry."

He nodded almost imperceptibly. He took a breath and then another. "I put it away, shut it out of my mind, didn't deal with it. I never talked to anyone about it—except you. Five years ago."

Her eyes widened. "You never—?"

"No. I shut it all out." There it was, the sharp hard edge. She could hear it. It was the way he always shut people out.

He bent his head. "But I couldn't shut you out." His voice was ragged. A faint smile touched his beautiful mouth.

"You certainly did," Daisy reminded him. She remembered his words all too well.

Alex had the grace to grimace. "I tried," he allowed. "Because you got under my skin. Made me feel things that scared the hell out of me."

"What?" Daisy blinked, confused.

"I was…falling in love with you—even back then, that first night." He pulled a hand out of his pocket and rubbed it against the back of his neck. "I was falling in love with you," he repeated, wonderingly, as if he was amazed he could admit it not only to her but to himself. "And it scared me to death. When you started talking about it like it was a good thing—loving—all I could think was, 'I've got to get out of here. I'll destroy her, too.'" His tone was harsh, anguished. And when she looked close she could see his eyes glistening. He blinked rapidly, then gave a quick shake of his head. "So I did." He swallowed. "Hell of a lot safer that way."

Daisy digested that. Drew in a breath, then another, and cocked her head, then asked him gently, "Was it?"

A corner of his mouth quirked up. "It was until I ran into you again back in September. Then, short answer—no. You're under my skin. I can't get rid of you. Wherever I go, wherever I am, there you are." He made it sound awful, but Daisy suddenly couldn't stop smiling.

Despairing, Alex shook his head. "I couldn't get you out of my mind, though God knows, I tried.

I told myself I needed a woman who didn't make me feel all the things you made me feel. But you must have noticed, I couldn't stay away."

"Every time I thought I'd seen the last of you, you came back," Daisy realized. "It made me nervous."

"Because of Charlie?"

"Partly. But really, I suppose, because I'd…never quite got over you." She didn't want to admit it, but if they were being honest, she owed him that. The heat of his gaze was warming her, making her tingle all the way to her toes. At the same time she was still trying to get a grip on the notion that five years ago he'd been falling in love with her, too.

"I wanted you as soon as I saw you again," he told her.

"On your terms."

"Hell, yes. Safer that way. And Caroline was safe. I never felt for her the tiniest bit of what I feel for you. I never wanted her. Never missed her. I knew I could live without her. I can't live without you."

"Alex." She touched his cheek with her palm and he turned his face to press his lips into it, his kiss making her shiver.

"I couldn't ask her to marry me," he admitted. "I was going to, but I never could."

"You must have realized she needed someone else."

He reached up a hand to press her palm against his cheek. He looked down into her eyes, his full of an emotion she'd never dared hope to see there. "Yeah, maybe that was it." He gave a self-deprecating laugh. "No, damn it. I was still in love with you."

Daisy stared at him in astonishment.

"And then I discovered Charlie."

"And you wanted Charlie."

"Yes. I love Charlie," Alex said with an intensity that made her believe it. "Not just because he reminds me of Vass, though God knows he does. I love him because he's yours. And mine. Because he's bright and inquisitive and fun and just knowing he's alive gives me joy." He shook his head slowly. "And I would give my life for him—and for you. I will go to the ends of the earth for you. I will slay dragons for you. I will get hurt for you. I swear it, Daisy." There was wonder in his voice.

Daisy opened her mouth, then closed it again. She didn't know what to say. Her eyes brimmed. So did her heart. Dear God, she'd loved this man for years, but never more than she loved him now, now that he had discovered the love he was capable of, the love he was willing to dare to share.

He reached out and touched her cheek, stroking away a tear she didn't even know was there. Then he wrapped his arms around her and drew her close, let her feel the pounding of his heart, the warmth of his love, the shelter of his embrace.

She leaned against him, letting herself sink into him, loving his strength, his steadiness. She rested her head in the crook between his shoulder and his chin.

"I would have been here sooner," Alex went on. He spoke softly, his lips against her hair. "But I didn't think you probably wanted to talk to me again after what you said the last time."

Daisy raised her eyes to look up at him, feeling guilty. "I didn't know—"

But Alex shook his head. "No, you were right. It was my problem. You gave me a reason to confront it, to deal with it. And I needed to before I could come back. So I did. I had to go to Paris for work anyway. It was a commitment. I spent ten days there. Then I went to see my parents."

Daisy took a quick look into his eyes.

He bent his head, held her closer. "We've…barely talked in years. It was, I suppose, easier for all of us that way. Not to be reminded."

Daisy slid her arms around his back, holding him close, feeling the tension in him.

He cleared his throat, scuffed his boot in the snow, then pulled back a little so he could look down into her eyes. "They're both in Greece these days. Not together. My mother's divorced a third time. My dad is still buried in his books. But I...talked to both of them. About Vass. About... what happened, about what I thought. They were shocked. They had no idea." His eyes were brimming again. He shook his head. "I'm glad I went. And I...expect I'll see them again." He hesitated. "I told them about you...and Charlie. They'd like to meet you both someday...if you're agreeable."

"Of course," Daisy said faintly, her heart spilling over with love for him, thrilled that he'd taken the step to reconnect with his parents, delighted that they might all now find a beginning to their healing.

Alex pressed a kiss into her hair. "Thank you."

Then he drew back and dug into the pocket of his jacket. "Will you give this to Charlie?" He took out a small silver Matchbox car and handed it to her. "I have real Christmas presents for him, but he's got them already. I left them with Cal."

"Cal?" She stared at him in wonder. "You've never even met Cal."

"I have now. I went to your place from the airport. You weren't there. I didn't know where you were. I thought you might be with him."

"How do you know where he lives?"

"I told you once before—" Alex's mouth quirked "—the internet is a wonderful thing."

Apparently it was. "But I wasn't there."

"No," Alex said. "But he knew where you were."

"And he told you?" That didn't sound like Cal. He was generally very protective.

"After he'd threatened me within an inch of my life. Said I'd be sorry if I hurt you. And I believed him. I liked him. And...I don't ever want to hurt you, Daze." His voice was rough and warm and intense.

And he wasn't hurting her, he was killing her, Daisy thought desperately. She looked down at the tiny car in her hand. Without having to be told, she knew what it was.

"The car you fought over," she said.

He nodded. "It was Vass's. He gave it to me before...before he died." Alex choked on the words. "I've carried it with me ever since."

"Your hair shirt?" Daisy asked gently.

"I didn't think so then, but yes, it was. I lived with the guilt a long time. I might have lived with it forever—without you."

"Oh, Alex." She nestled close again.

"Charlie should have it. He doesn't need to know its past. Only that it's for him—a gift from the uncle he'll never know. Vass—" Alex swallowed "—would have loved him."

Daisy blinked furiously, her fingers tightening around the tiny car. "Yes." She tucked it into the pocket of her jacket. "Oh, yes."

"I have something for you, too." He fished in his other pocket and pulled out a small box, the sort that jewelry came in. A ring box?

Daisy's heart hammered furiously. More manipulation? Or were they past that?

Alex held it out to her. "This is for you. I saw it at a little shop in Paris and I thought of you. Of us. It's the way I'd like us to be." He looked into her eyes and pressed it into her palm, then closed her fingers over it. Snowflakes dusted his dark lashes, settled on his midnight hair. He smiled gently. "I love you, Daisy. I hope someday you believe it."

Then he drew away from her, turned and set off through the snow.

Numbly, Daisy stared after him. *What?*

He was just going to leave her here? He was going to tell her he loved her, give her his heart, then walk away?

No insistence? No demand? No renewed proposal?

She looked down at the tiny box in her hand, then fumbled to open it. Inside was a silver necklace—real silver, unlike the Porsche—of two interlocking, entwined open hearts.

I thought of you, he'd said. *Of us.*

Two open hearts entwined.

Daisy bit down on her lip. Her fingers trembled. She clutched the box with the necklace in one hand and her camera bag in the other and broke into a run. "Alex! Alex, wait!"

He stopped, turned. Looked at her, half stricken, half hoping. She recognized that look now. She skidded to a halt bare inches in front of him, blinking furiously into the sun, into the dawning hope in those beautiful pale green eyes. "Ask me."

He frowned. "Ask what?"

"You know what!"

He raised a brow. A corner of his mouth quivered, almost smiled.

"Ask," Daisy demanded.

Then he took a breath. "Will you let me love you?" he asked. "Forever?"

"Yes." She threw her arms around him.

"Will you love me?" he asked as she kissed him. His voice was suspiciously hoarse.

"Yes!" She breathed the word against his lips.

"Will you marry me, Daze?" He barely got the words out because now he was kissing her back.

"Yes, Alex. Oh, yes, yes. Yes."

Daisy didn't miss Charlie that night as much as she'd thought she would. She took Alex home and didn't even open the other Christmas present he'd brought her from Paris.

She put on her necklace—or, rather, he put it on for her. Then she took him upstairs to her bedroom. There, slowly, he took off her sweater, her jeans, her shirt, her socks. Then he lowered her to the bed, and, smiling, began to take off everything else she wore.

Everything but the necklace. Daisy wouldn't let him take off that. But the rest—oh, yes. She shivered with pleasure at the way his fingers traced the lines and curves of her body, the way his lips followed and his tongue, as well.

When he unfastened her bra and slipped it off her shoulders, then bent his head to kiss her breasts, she lifted her hands and threaded them in the silky softness of his hair.

Alex kissed his way across her breasts, laved her nipples, made her tremble with longing. Then, smiling at her reaction, he dropped kisses down the line between her breasts, on down to her navel and beyond. And Daisy quivered with need for him.

"Alex!" She squirmed when he peeled her panties down, tossed them aside, then ran his fingers back up her calves, then her thighs, then touched her—there. "Wait. My turn. You're overdressed."

He lifted his head and smiled. "Am I?"

"Oh, yes." And then Daisy set about unwrapping the Christmas present she wanted more than anything—him.

"I love you," she whispered as she tugged his sweater over his head. "I've never forgotten doing this." She tossed his sweater on the bedside chair, then quickly disposed of the buttons of his shirt.

"You're faster at that than I remember." Alex kept his hands at his sides as he watched her, but there was a flame of desire in his eyes.

"Practice," Daisy said, beginning to work on the zip of his jeans.

"Practice?" Alex frowned.

"Charlie couldn't always dress himself."

He grinned, then sucked in a quick breath when she made quick work of the zipper and her fingers found him. He swallowed hard, then shrugged off his jeans and came to her on the bed, settled next to her, stroked his hands over her with an almost hesitant wonder.

And Daisy felt the same. "I love you," she whispered, glorying in being able to say it, to acknowledge it, and to know that he wanted to hear the words.

"I know. But not as much as I love you," he said, a tremor in his voice and another in the hands that stroked her sensitive skin.

"I'll show you," she insisted, and rolled onto her back, drawing him on top of her, wrapping herself around him.

"And I'll show you," Alex countered, teasing, tasting, touching. He was so exquisitely gentle, yet possessively so. His fingers found her, knew her, parted her. And then he slid in. "Daze!" His body tensed, froze. And then—at last—he began to move.

"Alex!" Her nails dug into his buttocks. Her head thrashed on the pillow. Her body tightened around him. He made her shiver, he made her quiver, he made her shatter. And he shattered right along with her, his face contorting, his body going rigid, then collapsing to bury his face against her neck.

She stroked his sweat-slick back, then turned her head and kissed his ear and along the whisker-roughened line of his jaw.

When at last he lifted his head it was to look down into her eyes with wonder. "Why did it take me so long to realize?" he murmured, sounding awestruck.

Daisy shook her head. She didn't need to ask why anymore. She had the answer she needed. "I'm just glad you did."

He rolled onto his back then and pulled her on top so that she rested her head on his chest and felt the gallop of his heart beneath her cheek. Softly, rhythmically, Alex stroked her hair.

Daisy didn't know how long they lay like that. She might have slept a little. She thought he did. But when they roused and began to touch, to love again, he raised his head from the pillow and peered down his nose at her. "Is this the sort of match you try to make?" he asked, giving her his heart with his eyes.

Daisy returned his gift full measure. But then she shook her head no.

"It's better," she told him, rising up to meet his lips, to love him, to share the wonder once more.

* * * * *

Mills & Boon® Large Print
May 2013

BEHOLDEN TO THE THRONE
Carol Marinelli

THE PETRELLI HEIR
Kim Lawrence

HER LITTLE WHITE LIE
Maisey Yates

HER SHAMEFUL SECRET
Susanna Carr

THE INCORRIGIBLE PLAYBOY
Emma Darcy

NO LONGER FORBIDDEN?
Dani Collins

THE ENIGMATIC GREEK
Catherine George

THE HEIR'S PROPOSAL
Raye Morgan

THE SOLDIER'S SWEETHEART
Soraya Lane

THE BILLIONAIRE'S FAIR LADY
Barbara Wallace

A BRIDE FOR THE MAVERICK MILLIONAIRE
Marion Lennox

0413 Rom LP

5